KILKENNY

KILKENNY

LOUIS L'AMOUR

BANTAM BOOKS
NEW YORK • TORONTO • LONDON • SYDNEY • AUCKLAND

KILKENNY

*A Bantam Book / published by arrangement with
the Author
Bantam edition / June 1983
Louis L'Amour Hardcover Collection / October 1986*

ISBN 0-553-06294-8

Published simultaneously in the United States and Canada

---

*Bantam Books are published by Bantam Books, a division of Bantam
Doubleday Dell Publishing Group, Inc. Its trademark, consisting of
the words "Bantam Books" and the portrayal of a rooster, is Registered
in U.S. Patent and Trademark Office and in other countries. Marca
Registrada. Bantam Books, 1540 Broadway, New York, New York
10036.*

PRINTED IN THE UNITED STATES OF AMERICA

0   9   8   7   6   5   4   3

KILKENNY

SOUTHEASTERN
UTAH
Countour interval 400 feet

Scale of Miles

0 1 2 3 4 5

Duck
Lake

Indian Creek

BLUE MOUNTAINS

Valley of the
Whispring Wind

Twin Peaks

The Causeway

Mule Can

Natural
Arch

Cliff
Dwelling

Mancos Jim
Butte

Wash

Dry

Black Steer
Knoll

Carson

Brushy Basin

Horsehead

Pinenut
Knoll

Butts Canyon

Whiskers

Draw

Cottonwood Creek

Carpenter

Westwater Creek

xas Cany
Flat

North Fork

KR Ranch

COMB RIDGE

Comb Wash

Butler Wash

BLACK MESA

Jones
Well

Map by Alan & William McKnight

ONE

To Clifton House on the Canadian came a lone rider on a long-legged buckskin. He was a green-eyed man wearing a flat-crowned, flat-brimmed black hat, black shirt and chaps. The Barlow & Sanderson Stage had just pulled in when the rider came out of the lava country, skirting the foothills of the Sangre de Cristos.

He was riding easy when they first saw him but his horse was dust-coated and the sweat had dried on him. The man had a tear in his shirt sleeve and a bloody bandage on his side. He rode directly to the stable and dismounted, caring first for his horse.

Only then did he turn and glance toward the House. He wore two tied-down guns. Pulling his hat lower he crossed the hard-packed earth and entered the house. "I could use some grub," he said, "a meal now and supplies to go."

"We got anything you need. We're feedin' the stage crowd now. Go on in."

He paused at the door and studied the room before going in. There were six passengers from the stage. Two women and four men, and there were a few riders from the valley roundup and three men from a trail herd crew. Face by face he studied them. Only then did he seat himself.

The tall girl from the stage lifted her eyes and looked across the table at him, her eyes alive with curiosity as she saw the bloody bandage. None of the men appeared to notice anything, and she filled her cup again and tried her coffee. It was hot, black, and strong.

1

Her eyes went again to the man in black. He had removed his hat when he seated himself and she noticed that his hair was black and curly. He was a lean, powerfully built man, probably larger than he looked while seated. Her eyes trailed again to the bandage.

"You . . . you've hurt yourself!" she exclaimed. "Your shoulder!"

Embarrassed and irritated, he glanced up. "It's a scratch," he said hastily. "It's all right."

"It looks like more than a scratch to me," she persisted. "You had better have it cared for."

"Thanks," he said, his voice a shade grim now, "I shall."

There was silence for a few minutes, and then from down the table somebody said, "Don't yuh wished yuh was scratched, Ike? Mebbe the lady would fix it for yuh."

The tall man flushed slightly but said nothing, but from down the table came a new voice. "Whatever it was scratched him," the voice said, "it looks like it hit him runnin' away!"

The dead silence that followed saw the tall man turn pale and cold. He lifted his head, his green eyes going down the table to the man who had spoken. He was a tough, handsome youngster with a look of eager recklessness about him. "If you were jokin'," the tall man said, "say so."

The man beside the tall man ducked suddenly and rolled off the bench, while others drew back from the blond young man. The youngster got slowly to his feet. "I wasn't jokin'," he said, with a faint sneer. "It looks to me like you was runnin' away."

As he spoke he went for his gun, and what happened then was seen with utter, piercing clarity by all who watched. The tall man seemed deliberately to wait, to hesitate the split second it took for the blond young man's hand to strike the butt of his gun. Then he palmed his own gun and shot.

The blond man staggered, his gun, half-drawn when the shot struck him, slid back into the holster. The man backed up, sat down, and rolled over on his face, coughing blood and death.

For an instant the room was still, broken by the young woman. She stared with horror at the tall man. "You . . . you *murderer!*" she cried, her lips twisting.

The tall man drew back slightly, his gun still in his hand. From one man to the other, he looked. "You saw it. He asked for it. I didn't want to kill him. I wasn't hunting for trouble when I came here. I was just tryin' to eat a quiet meal. What did he want to jump me for?"

Nobody spoke for a few seconds and then an older man said quietly, "Don't blame yourself, stranger. The boy has been huntin' for trouble ever since he killed a man in Texas."

"That won't make no diff'rence for yuh," another man said. "When Tetlow hears yuh've shot his boy, he'll never rest until he nails yore hide on the fence."

The tall man drew back and holstered his gun. "I'm not looking for trouble," he said. "I'll take my supplies and leave. Just you remember that," he added. "I'm not lookin' for trouble."

He sat down at the table and using his left hand he made two sandwiches from meat and bread. Wrapping them in a kerchief, he shoved them into his chaps pocket, backed away from the table, turned and walked into the other room. Tom Stockton was waiting for him. On the counter was a sack filled with supplies. "There it is, son. I seen it, an' it was a fa'r shootin' if there ever was one. Take this stuff, an' welcome."

"Thanks," the tall man hesitated, "but I want to pay."

"I'll take it hard," Stockton said grimly. "Yuh take this an' go along. It's little enough I can do for *Kilkenny!*"

Although he hissed the last name gently, the tall man looked quickly around. "Don't say that name!" he said. "Don't mention it!"

"*I* won't," Stockton replied, "but there's others in there may. Johnson," he nodded toward the dining room, "is from the Live Oak country. He may know yuh."

"Thanks again." Kilkenny turned, then he paused. "This Tetlow—who is he?"

Tom Stockton leaned his big hands on the counter and his face was grave. He had established Clifton House in 1867 to serve the roundup crowds and it had become a stage station. Since then and before he had seen much of the West and he had known most of it before. He knew this young man both by reputation and by intuition, and he liked him, and knowing this man and knowing Tetlow—

"It couldn't be worse. He's from Tennessee, Kilkenny, with all that means. He's the old bull o' the woods, a big, hard old man, but aristocratic, intelligent, smart, and a politician. Worse, he comes of a feuding family. He'll not rest until he gets you, or you him."

Kilkenny nodded. "I see. What's he doing here?"

"He's not here, not yet. But he's comin'. South of here on the flat he's got six thousand head of cattle. That's the second herd. The first one was four thousand head. He's got two more herds comin'."

"He'll need a lot of land for that many cattle," Kilkenny said. "I hope he's got it spotted."

"If he hasn't," Stockton replied, "he'll get it." He jerked his head. "That one, the one you shot. He was tall-talkin' around here. Said if they didn't get the land any other way they knew how they could get it. And he slapped his gun when he spoke."

"It's been done," Kilkenny said.

Stockton nodded gloomily. "Which makes it mighty tough on the little man who can't hire gunmen. Knowin' somethin' about Tetlow, however, I'd say that he wouldn't fall back on guns until politics failed. He's a smooth one, an' like I said—he's a politician."

To the high valleys then, came a lone rider, a man who rode with the caution born of riding long on strange trails in a land untamed and restless with danger.

The Indian Wars were largely of the past, although there were still the Sioux, the Cheyenne, Nez Percé and the Apache with fight left in them, but on the land from which the Indian had been driven or from which he was being driven the white man had not found peace—or at best an uneasy peace when men rode with guns at hand and eyes alert for danger.

Cattle had come to replace the buffalo, and then bolder men had pushed their herds into the mountain valleys, valleys lush with grass that fattened cattle amazingly fast, and as these valleys began to be settled, some men drifted to the high meadows among the peaks.

Lonely, largely overlooked, but excellent grazing in spring, summer and early fall, the valleys were the last land to be taken. It was to one such valley that Kilkenny rode, and when he drew up and looked around him, he made his decision. This was the home he had been seeking, on this land would he stay.

Riding on, he studied the valley. To right and left lay towering ridges that walled the valley in, and to the east other peaks lifted, and west the valley swung hard around and at one corner the wall was broken sharply off to fall sheer away for more than six hundred feet. Kilkenny paused long upon the lip, looking out over that immeasurable distance toward the faraway line of the purple hills. It was then that he first became conscious of the sound, a faint scarcely discernible whispering. Holding himself erect, he listened intently. It was the wind! The whispering wind!

Wind among the tall pines, among the rocks and the erosion-gnawed holes, a sound such as he had never heard, a sound like far off music in which no notes could be detected, a sound so strange that he could not stop listening. He turned then in his saddle and looked back over the valley he had found. At least two thousand acres! Grassy and lush with growth, water aplenty, and that whispering! The Valley of the Whispering Wind!

It was a strange thing to find this place now, this place where he knew he could find happiness, the place from which he would not move again. He had told himself that before he realized what it might mean, and when he did know, he nodded his head as if at last he could be sure.

Yes. Here he would stop. Here he would cease being the restless drifter that he had become, a man fleeing from a reputation, fleeing from the reputation of a killer. But in this place he would stay, and he would find peace—if they let him.

There was always the chance that some stranger from the plains might drift into the country and recognize him as Kilkenny, yet he was fortunate in that few men knew him well, and most descriptions of him were mistaken. There was always the chance of such a killing as the affair at Clifton's. That man had not even known who he was, just a trouble-hunting kid wanting to prove how tough he could be. But that was over, and it was miles away over some of the roughest land in the world. And here he would stay.

His fire was a lonely gleam in the vast darkness of the valley, and in the morning he saw where the cougars had come down from the rocks to investigate, and once he found the tracks of a grizzly. Killing a deer for food, he started in then to work. Living on the ground under the stars, he laid the foundations of his home, choosing flat stones from the talus of the ridges, carefully laying the foundation and the floor. When a space for three rooms was carefully laid, he crushed limestone, and with sand made a crude mortar and began building the walls from selected chunks of rock.

It was slow, bitterly hard work, but he enjoyed it, and during that first month in the high meadow there was no sound or sight of anything man had done but what he did with his own hands. While he worked, he thought carefully of what he would do now. The house was nearing completion, and he had cleaned the waterholes and walled up the spring near the cabin.

Soon he must go to a settlement for supplies and ammunition. He felt a curious hesitancy about that, for he had no desire to go. Always now he found himself remembering the queer horror on that girl's face after he had shot Tetlow. True, she did not understand what it meant. She was new to the West. Still, it was not pleasant to have one looked at with such horror.

Who was she? She was without doubt beautiful—very beautiful.

As beautiful as . . .? He shook his head. No. There was no other like Nita, and there would be no other like her.

On the first day of the seventh week in the high meadow, Kilkenny saddled up and started for town. He knew nothing of the place. Horsehead, they called it, and while riding toward it he had heard it mentioned, but no more. He did not even know how to get there, but must find his way through the canyons.

Horsehead sprawled in lazy comfort along both banks of a creek called Westwater, and the town's main street crossed the creek at right angles. The ancient stone stage station, a veteran of Indian fighting and earlier Mormon settlement, stood near the east bank of the creek. It was a low-roofed, single-storied building with an awning that projected eight feet from the roof and offered shelter to a couple of initial-carved benches polished by the seats of many breeches.

Above the doorway was a crude sign lettered *Horsehead: Stage Station. Eat & Drink.* Drinks were occasionally served over the tiny six-foot bar, but no meals had been served for six years. East of the stage station was the two-story Westwater Hotel & Saloon, and it was here the elite usually ate. East of the hotel in lazy comfort were the Harness Shop, Eli Putnam, Prop., the Barber Shop, the office of Robt. Early, Lawyer, and a scattering of other structures steadily declining in height until they reached the usual Last Chance Saloon.

Opposite the stage station was the sheriff's office and jail. The town marshal had a desk in the same office but no love was lost between the two men. Alongside the sheriff's office and facing the hotel was the assayer's office, and beyond it in a row were the Pinenut Saloon, the Emporium, the real estate office and then the Diamond Palace Saloon & Gambling Hall and a trail of further buildings.

West of the creek was a section of town all by itself, and one largely ignored by the businesses and citizens who lived on the east bank. A grove of trees, mostly cottonwoods but mixed with willows and a scattering of others, occupied the immediate bank and partly shaded the bridge. Beyond the trees were the corrals and wagon yards of the livery stable, and then the huge and sprawling stable itself. Beyond the stable was the bunkhouse, which was a place for casual sleeping, and possessing no rooms, but merely a dozen tiers of bunks, two high, and a few tables.

Alongside the bunkhouse was Savory's Saloon, but it was not considered very savory. This was the "tough" place of the town. A long, narrow building with a long bar and a good many tables, it had been ever since its construction a hangout for the town's tough element as well as for occasional drifting cowhands.

Across the dusty street and beyond the usual line of hitching rails and opposite the corrals was the office of Doc Blaine, tall, undeniably handsome, forty, of mysterious background, but without doubt, gossip had it, the best surgeon west of the Rio Grande. Doc Blaine was usually drunk, but during his occasional periods of lucidity he removed bullets, patched knife-wounds and bottle-cuts, or otherwise administered to the well-being of the town's wrong side. His office was, obviously, strategically located near the scene of most of the shootings, cuttings, and beatings, their source being anywhere along the street in front of the bunkhouse or Savory's.

West of the Doc's was Dolan's, a resort with one pool table, several card tables, too much cigar and cigarette smoke and drinks served from another tiny bar. Yet Dolan's was not a saloon.

Those who frequented the place were an interesting cross-section of the town. Dolan was an ex-soldier, a former sergeant of cavalry and a veteran of the Mexican, Civil, and Indian wars.

Beyond Dolan's to the west were two deserted buildings and then the blacksmith shop, and beyond it, the canyon. This last was a deep slash in the rock of the mesa, deeper than the nearby creek, but waterless except for the brief rushes of water following heavy rains. This was also bridged.

Lance Kilkenny rode down from the hills into the east side of town, riding on until he reached the stage station, where he dismounted and tied the buckskin at the hitch rail. Pausing there, he took out the makings and rolled a smoke, scanning the town with careful eyes, alert to any attention he might be getting and curious about the town itself.

Ducking under the hitch rail he settled his hat back in place and glanced at the loafer standing in front of the stage station. "Nice little town you've got here," he suggested.

The loafer glanced at him out of the corners of his eyes, then at the two low-tied guns. "I reckon," he agreed, wiping the back of his hand across his mouth. "You seen Dolan?"

"Don't know him," Kilkenny said. "Who's he?"

The loafer stretched, then jerked his head toward the west side of town. "A good man to know if yuh figure to stick around." Turning, the man sauntered away.

His brow puckered slightly, Kilkenny watched him go, then turned east toward the hotel. He was a tall man, well over six feet, with wide shoulders, thick and powerfully shaped. His hips were lean and his waist small. When he walked, it was less the rider's walk than the woodsman's. Turning into the Westwater Hotel, he sought out the dining room and dropped to a seat at a table near the back of the room. He glanced curiously at the menu, then looked again, for here in this cow country hotel was a menu that would have favored any cafe in Paris.

He turned the page, then turned it back again. One facing page listed the usual cow country meals, but on the other was a French menu listing at least fifty dishes!

"Surprised?"

Kilkenny glanced up to see a square-shouldered man of medium height standing above him. On the man's vest was a sheriff's badge. Kilkenny's eyes went from the badge to the rough-hewn features. The mustache was white, trimmed, and clean. The eyes were a cool blue, now faintly quizzical and amused.

"Yes," he responded, "I sure am. Sit down, Sheriff."

"Thanks." The sheriff dropped into the chair across the table. "My name's Leal Macy. Whenever a stranger wearing two guns comes into town I try to make his acquaintance."

Kilkenny looked at the menu again, and when the waitress approached he said, "I'll have the Paupiettes de Veau Provençal, an' tell your chef I'll have nothing but Madeira in the sauce."

Macy grinned, but his eyes were alert and curious. "Ernleven will like that. The man's a marvel with food and takes it as a personal favor if anyone orders from the French side of the menu. An' yuh'd be surprised how many do. The West," he added, "is made up of a lot of odd characters. I went over the trail from Texas once with two university men in the crowd. One from the Sorbonne and one from Heidelberg."

"Yeah." Kilkenny was alert now. If the sheriff had been over the trail there was scarcely a chance he had not heard of Kilkenny— unless it had been among the earliest trips. "The promise of a new country attracts men from everywhere."

"Going to be around long?" The question was casual.

"Permanent."

Macy looked at him again, more carefully. "We need good men. This is good country. Planning on ranching?"

"Uh-huh. In a small way."

"Located yet?"

"Yeah."

There was a moment of silence, then Macy asked, "Might I ask where? I haven't seen you around before."

Kilkenny nodded with his head toward the northwest. "Over there." He turned his green eyes toward the sheriff. "An' I haven't seen you around before, either. However, Macy, let's get this straight. As sheriff you've seen these guns I pack an' you're probably wonderin' what all I want around here. I want to be let alone. I've picked the loneliest place I can find and I've holed up there. Unless something unusual happens, I'll be in town no more than once a month after I get located. I don't hunt trouble, an' I've never been drunk in my life. Sometimes," he added, "it doesn't pay to get drunk an' forgetful. You'll have no trouble with me. I figure to run a few cattle and to mind my own affairs—but I want to be let alone."

"Fair enough," Macy nodded agreeably. "Know anybody in town?"

"Not a soul. And I have spoken to only one man before you. He volunteered the information that I should see Dolan."

Leal Macy felt a little shock of excitement go through him and he looked again at this tall man, measuring him, wondering. Then he said, more carefully, "If I were you, I'd not see him. Not now, anyway. Let it ride until your next trip. Dolan," he added, "is a tough case, and around that place of his you'll find most of the rag ends and bobtails of the country. Drifters, rustlers, gunmen, outlaws, and just no-goods."

"Is he on the rustle?"

"If he is, nobody ever caught him at it. Dolan's an ex-army sergeant. A good fighting man, shrewd, and very able. He rode with Sheridan."

"So did I," Kilkenny replied quietly.

He looked up suddenly, hearing the door close, and for a long moment he made no move. In the door stood the young woman of Clifton's and her eyes were on him, wide with recognition. He arose quickly. "How do you do, ma'am? I hope you've been well?"

Her eyes held his, filled with uncertainty. Then she nodded and crossed to a table not far away. Macy said nothing but he was obviously interested.

The waitress returned and served Kilkenny's meal and at his suggestion brought Macy a cup of coffee. The waitress hovered by the table and when Kilkenny glanced up, she said, "The chef says the sauce is *always* with genuine Madeira."

Kilkenny grinned. "Macy, I may be in town more than I planned. If the food is going to be this good, I can't stay away. A man gets tired of his own cookin'."

The door opened again and three dusty cowhands came in and dropped into chairs around a table. All three were unshaven and had obviously been riding hard and long for they had that lean, hungry, wild look of men off the trail. One of them was a lumbering big fellow with fat cheeks and a thick neck, another had a scar along his cheekbone and the small finger missing from his right hand. The third man was a man of sandy complexion, almost white eyes and he wore his gun thrust into his waistband.

After seating themselves they let their eyes wander around the room, noting the sheriff and studying him carefully. If Macy was conscious of their attention he gave no evidence of it. Kilkenny came in for a share of their regard and the big man kept looking at him as if trying to recall where he had seen him before.

The food was excellent and the coffee black and strong. It was like paradise after the long days riding west, eating half-cooked meals in the lee of a cliff or near some wayside waterhole. From time to time he glanced up and twice he met the eyes of the girl from Clifton's. What, he wondered, was her name? Was she stopping here?

He hesitated, then put the question to the sheriff. "Thought you knew her," Macy said. "As a matter of fact, she's just out here from the East. She's a niece of Bob Early, the town's best lawyer. Her name is Laurie Webster.

"New to the West," he added, "but a fine horsewoman. The best I've seen except for Nita Riordan."

Kilkenny felt the shock clear to his heels. He held himself a minute, afraid to speak, and then he said carefully, "Who did you say?"

"Nita Riordan. She's got the KR spread, southwest of here. Runs the ranch herself, although she's got a foreman that knows his business. She rides astride like a Western woman. I hear she came from the Live Oak country, down near the Rio Grande."

"That right? The name sounded familiar, but I guess I was mistaken."

Macy chuckled good-humoredly. "Friend," he commented, "if you ever saw this girl you'd never forget her. Spanish and Irish, and beautiful! All woman, too, but one who can take care of herself. She handles a pistol like a man, and a Winchester, too. But no nonsense about her, and nobody makes her any trouble. That foreman of hers is like her shadow. He's a big Mexican, and I've seen him shoot heads off quail with his six-shooter."

"Been here long?"

"Not very. About seven or eight months. She came in here and bought out old Dan Marable, but since she took over you'd never know the place. She's built a big new house, new stables and has brought some new stock into the country. I'm afraid she'll have trouble now, though, with this new outfit comin' in."

Macy drank his coffee. "She's running cattle on that country south and west of town, clear back to Comb Ridge. It's good graze and she'll do all right if she doesn't have trouble with this new outfit."

When the sheriff had gone, Kilkenny's attention went to the girl at the nearby table. He hesitated, wanting to speak to her, wanting to explain. But the information Macy had given him crowded out all else.

Nita Riordan was here! Her brand was the KR, but he refused to let himself believe what that K might mean. Kilkenny and Riordan . . . but there were so many reasons why a particular brand might be used. Yet she would soon know he was here, and without doubt they would meet.

The big man across the room was watching him and whispering to his companions. Unmindful of what it might mean, he arose and crossed to Laurie Webster's table. "I beg your pardon, Miss Webster," he said, "but I would like to apologize for causing you any discomfort back down the trail. The fight was forced on me."

"I know. And can you ever forgive me? To have it happen right before me . . . it was awful. But I do understand that you had to do it."

"Thanks." He stepped back. "Maybe we'll see each other again."

He walked out, conscious of the eyes of the three men. It was bright and sunny in the street and there was a fresh smell of hay, dust, and warm lumber. It was time to get his supplies and go, yet he delayed, unwilling to leave so soon.

Suppose Nita came into town this morning? Suppose, even now, she was in one of the stores? Yet, if they did meet, what could he expect? He had to run away because he was afraid of what his guns might do to their love for each other, how inevitably he would some day be killed. At the time it had seemed the thing to do.

Through the plains country his name had become a legend, a mysterious rider whose gun skill compared with that of Hickok, Thompson, and Earp. He was said to be faster than Hardin, colder than Doc Halliday. Yet few knew him well enough to describe him, for he moved often and used many names.

Partly concealed by the awning post and the shade of a huge cottonwood, he saw the three men come from the hotel and mount their horses. All wore the 4T brand. He watched them ride out, then he crossed to the Emporium and bought the supplies he needed. He crossed the bridge to west town and drew up at the livery stable.

"Got a pack horse for sale?"

"See Dolan. He's the man with horses to sell."

Kilkenny hesitated. Dolan might know him. A lot of men had ridden with Sheridan, but the last thing he wanted was to be recognized in this town. Yet to pack the supplies he wanted he needed at least one more horse.

The man indicated the corrals. "He might sell that paint."

The fellow got up, taking his pipe from his mouth. He was a small man with work-hardened hands. "Seen the marshal yet?"

"Macy? Yes, I've seen him."

"He's the sheriff. I mean the marshal, Harry Lott. If you ain't seen him, you will. He aims to get the jump on strangers. Says the way to run a town is to keep it buffaloed."

"How do he and Macy get along?"

"They don't. Macy's a solid citizen."

The man still hesitated. "My name's Hammett. Tell you what I'll do. I'll see if Dolan has a pack horse to sell."

"It'll be a favor."

Kilkenny walked to the corral and studied the horses. They were not the kind to be found on any cattle spread, but chosen animals, the sort preferred by outlaws who needed speed and bottom. He had walked around the corner of the corral when a big, heavy-shouldered man strode down to where he had been standing and looked around. He had a long, hard-jawed face. He wore two guns tied down and he was roughly and carelessly dressed. On his vest was a badge.

Lott looked across the street toward Dolan's, then settled down to wait. Kilkenny rolled a smoke. Hammett came out of Dolan's and stopped on the step. Lott called to him and Hammett crossed the street. Kilkenny could hear their voices. "Where's the man who rode this horse?"

"He said something about getting a drink," Hammett said. "Stranger to me."

"What's he look like?"

"Looks all right. But nobody to monkey with. Looks mighty salty."

"He got to Savory's?"

"Didn't see. He ain't in Dolan's."

Lott walked past Hammett and headed for Savory's Saloon. Hammett watched him go, then caught up the buckskin's reins and brought him to Kilkenny. "Dolan said you could have the paint for fifteen bucks, but you'd better ride out of town until Lott gets over his sweat. He's drinkin' and huntin' trouble."

"Thanks." Kilkenny handed fifteen dollars to Hammett, then got into the corral and roped the paint. Putting on a halter and lead rope, he mounted his own horse and with a wave to Hammett, rode through the trees into the creek. He would avoid crossing the bridge in case the sound drew Lott back to the street.

At the Emporium he bought a pack saddle and loaded up, keeping a watchful eye out for Harry Lott. Irritably he realized he was only avoiding an issue that must soon be faced.

At a thunder of hoofs he turned to see a dozen riders charge into the street. A pistol bellowed, then another. They swung down in front of the Diamond Palace and the Pinenut and charged inside, yelling and laughing. The tall man in black who had led them remained in the street. With him was a wiry man, slender and gray-faced. His eyes seemed to be almost white.

The tall man bit the end from a cigar and Harry Lott came up the street. "Who made that racket?" he demanded. "Who was shootin'?"

The reply came, ice-cold and domineering. "Those were my men, Marshal, and the shooting was harmless. They will come to town often, and we will have no trouble. Understand?"

Harry Lott's eyes glowed. This man, Kilkenny saw, was a killer. Yet he saw more than that. The gray-faced man had moved to one side. The movement drew Kilkenny's attention and for the first time he saw the man's face in the sunlight. It was Dee Havalik.

In the Sonora cattle war his ruthless killings had won him the name of Butcher Havalik. Unassuming in appearance, he was deadly as a rattler and blurred lightning with a gun.

Harry Lott had not even noticed him. Lott was watching the older man, and Lott was in a killing mood.

Why he did it, Kilkenny would never know. Perhaps he wanted to see no man murdered. He spoke softly, just loud enough for Lott to hear. "Careful, Lott! The other one's Havalik!"

Lott stiffened at the name, and Kilkenny saw his eyes shift, then return to Tetlow. "And who are you?" Lott demanded of the older man.

"You mark well the name." The old man stood a little straighter. "I'm Jared Tetlow! And I've fifty riders, enough to sweep this town off the map!"

Harry Lott was no fool. And at that moment he saw the third man. It was the big man Kilkenny had seen earlier in the Westwater dining room. He was fifty yards away, only his face was rifle muzzle showing over the back of a horse. That rifle was leveled at Harry Lott.

It was a cold deck, and Lott knew it.

"Keep your men in line," he said, "and we'll have no trouble." Turning on his heel he walked toward the Emporium, slanting his eyes toward Kilkenny.

Tetlow and Havalik went inside. The man with the rifle loafed in front of the barber shop.

Lott studied Kilkenny suspiciously. "You saved my neck," he said. "They had me in a cross fire."

"I don't like to see a man murdered."

"I heard about Havalik." Lott had buck teeth and a heavy body. "Who are you?"

"I've been called Trent. Seems like a good name."

When he had packed his supplies he swung into the saddle and rode out of town, taking the route across the bridge, past Dolan's and turning right into the hills when he passed Savory's.

The tall old man with the autocratic manner was Jared Tetlow, father of the man he had killed at Clifton's! And such a man would be a desperate and implacable enemy. And this man commanded the guns of Dee Havalik!

TWO

Kilkenny rode west from Horsehead. The Valley of the Whispering Wind was almost due north but he had no intention of leaving a trail that could be easily followed.

One sight of Tetlow had indicated the nature of the man who would be his enemy. Once the cattleman knew the man who had killed his son was nearby he would not rest until that man was dead. Nor was Kilkenny unaware of the danger that lay in Harry Lott.

Several times he paused just over ridges to look back along his trail. As he suspected, he was followed. At dusk he turned into the head of Butts Canyon, riding down a switchback trail that was rarely used. He took his time entering and made sure there were visible tracks. Within the canyon it was black as a cavern, yet he trusted his horse, knowing the mountain-bred gelding would take him through safely. It was cool, almost cold at the canyon bottom.

At the first fork he rode into a narrow, cavernous passage that led back into the plateau to the northwest. He had no idea if there was any trail out, but it was a chance he must take.

When they had gone some distance up the branch canyon the buckskin pulled to the right. With carefully shielded matches Kilkenny studied the ground and found the buckskin had started into a trail apparently used by deer and wild horses. Swinging back into the saddle, he let the buckskin have his head. Nearly an hour later they emerged atop the mesa. A notch in the hills to the north promised a pass and he headed toward it.

The night was cool and the stars seemed amazingly close.

Several times he paused to rest his horses, and when traveling stuck to rocky ledges whenever possible. Toward daybreak he made dry camp in a clump of juniper, picketing his horses on a small patch of grass.

He made breakfast over a fire of dry and smokeless wood at daybreak, but before he moved out he took his glasses and from a nearby rock devoted fifteen minutes to a careful survey of the country. He saw no sign of life, no trail of smoke.

Mounting, he rode into wilder and even more lonely hills. It was a desolate land, a jumbled heap of uptilted, broken ledges, enormous basins, knifelike, serrated ridges and toppling towers of sandstone. The sun climbed and grew hot, weirdly eroded sandstone danced like demons in the heat-waved air. Dust devils moved mockingly before him, and the distant atmosphere gathered splendid blue lakes in distant bottoms.

Sweat stained his shirt and got into his eyes. The buckskin turned dark with sweat and the red dust that shrouded the junipers began to cover him, but still he rode north, knowing nothing of the waterholes, into a trackless and forbidding land.

For almost ten miles he rode across windswept rock where no trail could be followed, and then suddenly as though weary of the heights it had been following, the plateau ended in a series of vast, gigantic steps that descended for several miles, dropping little by little into a basin. Coming upon a wild horse trail, Kilkenny followed until he came to a small, blue, and beautiful lake where grew a few willows and cottonwoods. Here he watered his horses and rested, smoking a cigarette and relaxing.

It was dusk before he moved again, and now he turned east, for the Blues were abreast of him, and he found a wild horse trail that led across a great natural causeway into the Blues. He made camp at dark and only reached his valley in the early light of the following morning.

There was no evidence that anyone had been here in his absence. With coffee on, he went out and removed the saddles from the horses and rubbed both of them down. The buckskin was accustomed to this and stood patiently, but the paint was restive, uncertain of what this new master intended. But the scraping of the dry handful of grass was pleasing, and finally he grew still and waited, enjoying the ministrations.

After breakfast he sat on the step of the house and cleaned his guns, then went out and set several snares and deadfalls to trap small game. He had the hunted man's hesitancy to shoot unless absolutely essential and the knowledge that much game could be captured without it. Donning moccasins, he walked off down the valley until he was a mile away from the house, well knowing a time might come when he would want game close around him.

Long accustomed to the wild, lonely life, Kilkenny moved like an Indian, and he could live like one. Few men knew the wilderness better, and although he appreciated the towns and the comforts they offered, he had grown accustomed to living in the wilds and could do it. He knew the plants for their nutritional or medicinal value, knew how to make many kinds of shelters and utensils for camp use, and given a hunting knife, or even without one, he could survive anywhere.

He had chosen a quiet life now, away from the centers of action, but even here trouble was building. A less experienced man could see what was about to happen. Despite the ranches and permanent homes, Horsehead was in no sense a settled community. Many were drifters who had come to get away, often capable men, and fiercely independent. Yet most were poor men, running a few cattle, and starting from scratch. Into this country Tetlow had come with his great herds and dozens of hard-bitten riders. Good range was scarce, insufficient to support his huge herds and the cattle they now carried.

Tetlow was arrogant, sure that his success gave him the right to demand and control. The ranchers were stubborn men, resentful of this outsider. The situation could scarcely have been more explosive.

From his own ranch in the Valley of the Whispering Wind, Kilkenny found nothing in the situation to insure hope. Tetlow's manner to Lott showed the sort of man he was and that he would ride roughshod over all who got in his way.

Aside from the presence of Nita Riordan and the fact that he had killed Tetlow's son, Kilkenny's sympathies were with the small ranchers, the men who were building homes rather than empires. For one man to grow so large as Tetlow meant many men must remain small or have nothing. The proper level lay between the two extremes, and this was the American way.

Three years before Lance Kilkenny had taken the trail to the Live Oak country to help a friend. He had met Nita Riordan there, keeping a saloon inherited from her father. On the border and in outlaw country, she had elected to run the saloon herself when she found it impossible to sell. Jaime Brigo, the half-breed Yaqui who had been her father's friend, had been her strong right hand. From the moment their eyes met there had been no doubt in either her mind or that of Kilkenny. And then Kilkenny had drawn back.

There was no place in his established life pattern for a woman. No day could pass when he felt free from danger, and any woman who loved him would go through a thousand private hells, never knowing when he might be killed by some reputation-hunting gunman. Despite her acceptance of this, Kilkenny had gone away.

The following year they met again in the cedar breaks of New Mexico where Kilkenny had been trying to establish a home. Trouble had come again, and Nita in the midst of it. Now she was here, ranching in this wild country.

Had she believed that because of its loneliness it would draw him? Or had she given him up and started her own life? Or was there, the thought brought a chill, another man? For three days he worked, thinking of this, with increasing restlessness. He used his adze to shape a plow for the share he had picked up in Horsehead, and when it was completed he broke ground for a small corn and vegetable garden.

In the evenings he rode and studied the country, becoming more and more familiar with all the canyons and mesas. There was no such cattle country anywhere around Horsehead.

On the fourth day he saddled the buckskin at daybreak and took the trail down Mule Canyon. By the direct route he was nearing Horsehead by noon and he circled to enter town from the west.

A spring wagon was tied in front of the Emporium with a four-horse team hitched to it. The brands were 4T, the Tetlow brand. Down the street he saw three horses wearing the same brand. Beside them was a sorrel horse with three white stockings, branded KR.

He turned quickly to get off the street and went into the dining room of the Westwater Hotel. As he entered, a man with a square-cut face, iron gray hair and cool blue eyes looked up from his meal. His eyes quickened with interest and Kilkenny turned sharply away and seated himself at a table across the room.

The effort was useless, for the man with the gray hair crossed the room and sat down opposite him. Kilkenny liked the cool, self-possessed manner of the man, and the neatness of his clothing.

"My name is Dolan."

"I'm Trent."

"I've good cause to remember you, *Major*—Trent."

Kilkenny's expression did not change. He had ended the War Between the States as Major Kilkenny.

"I heard you were with Sheridan."

"You'd not remember me, but I've cause to remember you. There was a bit of a skirmish in a little Mississippi village and you came in with ten soldiers to drive out some guerrillas who were looting. You were outnumbered five to one and had to pull out."

"It was a rough go."

"There was a Union soldier lying wounded in a barn. He had been trying to fight them off for more than an hour before you rode into town. You heard about him after you had pulled out."

"I remember. Some village girl told me."

"Through heavy fire you rode back, fought off an attack with six guns, and when they broke in, killed three men with a Bowie knife before they broke and ran."

"Makes me sound a desperate character. Actually, it was mostly luck. They came into the darkness from the glare of the sun."

He studied Dolan. "You seem well informed."

"I was the soldier you carried out of there. But for you I'd be dead."

"You owe me nothing. It was the chance of war."

"Naturally, you'd feel that way." Dolan bit the end from a cigar. "This is a new country. We have two large cattle outfits, the KR and the 4T, and they will soon be fighting. The situation could become prosperous for us all."

"The 4T will spend money," Kilkenny said quietly. "That should increase prosperity. It won't make matters easier for the local rustlers. The 4T can take care of itself."

"Possibly."

"Dee Havalik is foreman for Tetlow."

Dolan stiffened and glanced sharply at Kilkenny. "Havalik? *Here?*"

"Better look at your hole card, Dolan. And"—some change in his voice made Dolan meet his eyes—"don't bother the KR."

Dolan studied Kilkenny with careful eyes. "That means you want it left alone? I suppose you wouldn't answer a question about it?"

"None."

"And Tetlow?"

"If he interferes with the KR, I'll see him."

Dolan waved his cigar irritably. "You don't leave me much."

Kilkenny smiled. "You look prosperous. If you're pushed you could always turn honest."

Dolan chuckled. "It's a desperate resort, but it may come to that." He got up. "Nevertheless, I'm your friend."

The 4T, or as it was called by its own people, the Forty, had established headquarters east of town. Tetlow sat by the wagon with his three sons, Phineas, Andy, and Ben. Jared had been talking of his dead son. "I'll find that man!" he promised. "I'll see him die!"

"Dad," Ben said quietly, "why hunt trouble? You know how the kid was. He was always on the prod. I don't blame anybody but the kid himself."

Tetlow's eyes flamed. "He was your brother, wasn't he?"

Dee Havalik squatted across from Tetlow. The older man wasted no time. With a stick he traced a crude map in the dust. "Carson runs cattle in Brushy Basin and east. He's got a small lake that holds through the dry spell. We'll go see him about sellin' out."

He looked up. "Dee, you're to come. Andy will stay with the cattle. We'll take Phin, Ben and two hands. Bring Cruz an' Stilwell. We'll go see this Carson."

Reluctantly, although he knew better than to object, Ben mounted his sorrel and followed the others. They rode swiftly until they drew up before the door of the small adobe house. A man of fifty came from the house wiping his hands on a handkerchief. "Light an' set, folks!" he invited. "Just got grub on, but there's some extry an' I can make more!"

"How much you want for this place?" Tetlow said abruptly.

Carson blinked. "This here?" He shook his head, smiling.

"Why, I like it here. I don't aim to sell. This here's the first home I ever had. I got me a few head of cattle an'—"

"How much?" Tetlow repeated brusquely. "Speak up, man! I've no time to waste!"

Carson's face stiffened, then his eyes grew wary as he looked from one to the other. "So that's the way of it? I wondered what yuh figured on doin' with that big herd. Well, I ain't sellin'. That's all there is to it."

"I'll give you a thousand dollars," Tetlow replied shortly. "Take it an' a horse an' git!"

"You're crazy!" Carson was angry now. "Why, I'm runnin' four hundred head o' fat stock! I got seven thousand acres o' land under my own use an' more to come! A thousand dollars? You're crazy!"

The men said nothing and there was absolute silence for the space of two minutes. Then Carson drew a step back, then another. He was afraid now, seeing the stern faces of these men. "One more chance," Tetlow said, "you get a thousand dollars an' a horse. Then you get clear out of the country."

"Go to hell!" Carson shouted. He wheeled and sprang for the door. A gun bellowed and he sprawled across the doorstep, his fingers grasping at the floor as if trying to drag himself inside.

"You seen it," Havalik's voice was casual, "he reached for a gun."

Ben's face was pale. He looked from his father to his brothers but their faces were blank, approving.

"Phin," Tetlow suggested, "you ride to town. Look up that Macy feller an' tell him what happened. Get on with it, now. We'll ride on over to Carpenter's place."

Phin swung his horse around and went off at a fast trot. With Jared Tetlow and Havalik in the lead, the rest of them took off for the Carpenter place. It was all of an hour's ride, and when they rode up to the door, Carpenter was walking up to the house with a bucket of milk.

Tetlow drew up, waving a hand around him. "What you want for this place? I'm buyin' land today."

Carpenter looked carefully at the riders and something in their eyes warned him. "Why, I don't know," he said cautiously, "I haven't thought about sellin'."

"Think about it then," Tetlow replied, "I need range and lots of it."

Carpenter hesitated. These riders had come from Carson's place and only a few hours ago he had been talking to Carson. The older man had been telling him of what he planned to do with his place, and both men had discussed the big herd of cattle and the rumor that more cattle were coming.

"What did Carson do?" Carpenter asked curiously. "Have you been over there?"

"Just came from there," Havalik offered. "We'll have that place, all right."

"Carson won't sell." Carpenter was positive. "We talked some last night."

"No," Tetlow agreed, "he won't sell. He won't have to. His place has been let go."

"Let go?" Carpenter was stunned. His eyes went from one to the other. Behind him he heard a sound inside the house, and he knew that sound. His wife was taking the scatter gun off the nails on the wall.

"Yeah, Carson won't be around any more. Cantankerous ol' cuss got right mean when we offered to buy him out. He grabbed for a gun. Well, what could we do?"

Carpenter looked at them, from one cold face to the other. "I see," he said slowly. "And if I don't sell? What happens then?"

Tetlow's horse stepped forward. "You'll sell," he said coldly. "What have you got here?" he sneered. "A little one-horse spread! Why, I've got thousands of cattle! I need all this range! You'll just putter along an' waste it! I'll put it to good use. I'll give you a thousand dollars an' you can keep your buckboard an' a team to fetch you an' your wife away from here."

"Free," the woman's voice spoke from the window of the cabin, "don't bother to talk to 'em any more. We got to strain that milk. Come on inside."

"You stay where you are!" Tetlow shouted, growing angry. "I ain't through with you!"

"You're through here." The woman's voice was cold. "This here's a Colt revolvin' scatter gun. She will fire four times. I reckon that's enough for all of you. Now ride off! You lift a hand to my man an' I'll start shootin'!"

Jared Tetlow stiffened, his face flooding with angry blood. "Easy, Dad!" It was Ben who spoke. "She means it."

"That's right," Havalik added, "she ain't foolin' an' at this range she could kill us all."

Tetlow cooled. That was right, of course. Anyway, they had done enough killing for one day. "All right!" he said crisply. "We're ridin'! But you make up your minds! We want this place!"

Wheeling, they rode away from the Carpenter place and back toward their own camp. "Dad," Ben interposed, "we'd better sit quiet until we see how the sheriff takes this Carson affair."

Tetlow snorted. "You saw him in the street! The man's gun-handy, all right, but we can talk to him! I know how to handle that sort!"

"That wasn't the sheriff, though," Ben persisted.

"Wasn't the sheriff?" Tetlow was growing angrier by the minute. Why did this son of his have to— "What do you mean? He wasn't the sheriff? You saw his badge, didn't you?"

"He was the town marshal, Dad. Not the sheriff. I hear the sheriff is a different sort, a very different sort."

Jared Tetlow scowled, but suddenly he was worried. Lott not the sheriff! He had taken for granted once he had seen the man that there was no need to worry. If the man couldn't be frightened he could be bought. Or enlisted.

"Why didn't you tell me?" he demanded. "You talk enough!"

"I started to tell you once, an' you wouldn't listen," Ben replied. "You never listen to me, an' it's time you did."

His father stared at him in amazement. "Since when did I take orders from a milksop?" he demanded. "You keep a still tongue in your head! I can make up my own mind!"

"All right," Ben replied shortly, "see if you can make up the sheriff's!" Wheeling his horse he rode rapidly off through the junipers. Jared Tetlow stared after him, scowling, his face black with the anger that always mounted quickly at any suggestion of resistance among his own people.

Nobody said anything, and the hands did not look at each other. They pushed on, riding swiftly toward the headquarters wagons.

Ben drew up when he was safely away from the cavalcade and watched them go. Where was all this going to lead? Did his father think everybody would cringe before him? That he could rule everyone with whom he came in contact? And that Dee Havalik! The man gave Ben the creeps.

Turning his sorrel, he rode on into town and left his horse at the hitch rail. He saw no sign of Phin anywhere. Either he had not yet found the sheriff or they had both started for the ranch. Suddenly recalling that the hotel was reported to have an excellent chef, he went up the steps and entered.

There were only two people in the cafe. A slender, attractive girl in a gray suit, and a man.

The man sat alone at a table facing the door. He wore a gray flannel shirt with a black silk neckerchief, black jeans, and he wore two guns tied low down on his thighs. His black, flat-crowned hat was on a hook nearby. As Ben entered, the man looked up, measuring him with careful eyes. Ben Tetlow never forgot that glance. It had in it something wary and unfathomable. It was the expression of a man who knew what it meant to command.

His eyes went again to the tall girl. She was more than attractive, she was really lovely. Suddenly, more than anything else in the world, he wanted to know her.

The man in black got to his feet and picked up his hat. He laid some coins on the table and glanced again at Ben. His glance now was friendly. "Good grub," he said, "you'll never find anything like that in a cow camp!"

Ben's smile was quick. "That's what I hear."

The tall man stopped by the girl's table. "Are you enjoying your stay, Miss Webster? I'm afraid there isn't much to do unless you like to ride."

"Oh, but I do! I love to ride!" Then she said quickly, "You have forgiven me, haven't you?"

He nodded, smiling. Then he excused himself and started for the door.

Ben Tetlow looked after the tall rider. "Forgive her for what?" he wondered.

He swallowed, then cleared his throat. "Seems like a nice fellow," he ventured.

She looked at him gravely with the expression of a little girl who has been taught not to talk to strangers. "Yes, he is nice, and

I'm so ashamed! I said some simply awful things to him! But you see, I had just come out west, and I saw him shoot a man."

"I know what you mean. It is never nice to see a man shot. Not even when he deserves it."

"This one did," Laurie said seriously. "I'm sure of it."

THREE

Lance Kilkenny had seen Ben Tetlow and surmised who he was and, walking outside to the boardwalk that ran along before the buildings, he frowned as he considered the situation.

There would be no avoiding the Tetlows or their riders. In the first place there were too many of them, and in the second the town was too small. What he wanted now was to find out what had been done, if anything. He was standing on the street when he saw Sheriff Macy come from his office in company with a tall, rather stooped young man. That this was Phin Tetlow he did not know, but he did see the 4T brand.

Why were the Tetlows calling on the sheriff? And Macy's face was stern. Kilkenny watched them pass, then turned and crossed the street to the sheriff's office and jail. An oldster with a handle-bar mustache sat with his feet on the desk. He nodded at Kilkenny. "Howdy! What can I do fer yuh?"

Kilkenny shrugged and smiled deprecatingly. "Nothing, really. Sort of loafin'." He jerked his head to the east. "Macy looked some upset."

The old jailer spat at the spittoon and scored dead center. "Ain't missed in ten year," he said, wiping the back of his hand across his mouth. "He should be upset. Carson had him an argyment an' tried to drag iron on Dee Havalik. The man must have been crazy!"

"Carson?" Kilkenny shook his head. "Don't know him."

"He's been batchin' out east o' here, got him a little two by four spread, few cows, good water. That young Tetlow said they went there to try to buy the place off him an' he ordered 'em off. When they tried to argy with him, he dragged iron an' Havalik shot him."

So it had started already! Kilkenny sat down and pushed his hat back on his head, stretching out his long legs. Wryly, he shook his head. "That Havalik," he said quietly, "I hear he's pretty slick with a gun."

"One o' the best," the jailer shook his head. "Carson must've been crazy."

"Anybody else see it?" Kilkenny asked innocently. "I mean anybody but the Tetlow outfit?"

"Now that you mention it, I don't reckon there was, but it sure don't make much diff'rence. Hombre like Tetlow wouldn't be startin' trouble with small fry like Carson. What would he want from him? Other way around, I wouldn't be s'prised."

Kilkenny shrugged, then he said ironically, "Yes, Carson might have tried to take Tetlow's herd away from him. He might have figured that fifty to one was about the right odds. Tetlow," Kilkenny added, "wouldn't think o' tryin' to steal Carson's land, or force him off it."

He got to his feet, noticing out of the corners of his eyes that the jailer was scowling thoughtfully. "Reckon I'll look around a mite. See you."

The sun lay lazily upon the town. A red hen pecked at some refuse lying in the dust, and a black and white shepherd dog flicked a casual tail at flies. Kilkenny strolled up to the Pinenut Saloon and rolled a smoke, leaning against the awning stanchion.

It was coming now and there would be no getting away from it. What would Leal Macy do? How much support would he get from this town? The jailer had seemed disposed to accept Tetlow's story without question, although Kilkenny's remarks might have planted doubt in his mind. Yet so many were willing to accept without question the word of any man who seemed to have money and power. Macy was not such a man, but could he get the local support necessary? Jared Tetlow had overnight altered the entire economic situation at Horsehead, becoming the largest single buyer to be found, and buying more than any three outfits in the area. Some of the local tradesmen would be afraid of running him out.

He heard the rattle of a buckboard and glanced up to see Doc Blaine come rolling down the street. He recognized the man from the black medical bag he carried and his manner. It could have been nobody but the town doctor. He pulled up in front of the Pinenut and got down, tying his team. "This isn't really necessary," he commented, faintly humorous, "these horses will stand in front of any saloon in the country. They know their master."

Kilkenny grinned, shifting his feet. "Have you been out to Carson's place?"

Blaine shook his head and looked curious. "What's the matter with him? That hard-bitten old coot isn't sick, is he?"

"He's dead. Dee Havalik shot him." Casually, Kilkenny repeated the story, watching Blaine's reaction. The doctor's eyes sharpened with attention and he nodded as though it followed some secret thought of his own.

"It begins to look," he said, "as if I may get a lot of unwelcome business."

"Could be." Kilkenny waited a minute, then asked, "Who lives near Carson's place?"

"Chap named Carpenter is his closest neighbor. Has a nice little place and a wife. They are good people—and they wouldn't take any nonsense."

"Any others?"

"Old Dan Marable. He sold out to this KR outfit, but kept a few acres for his own use, and then there's a family named Root. Man and wife and two young boys. They have about three or four hundred head down there, and the KR, of course."

"There may be more trouble."

Doc Blaine studied Kilkenny with alert, interested eyes. "You're looking ahead, my friend. What's your part in all this?"

"That," Kilkenny replied, "will be left to time. But I'm curious about Carson. You think he would draw a gun on a party of armed men?"

Blaine considered that. "No," he said finally, "he's no fool. He wouldn't put a hand near a gun with Dee Havalik around. And so far as I know, he never carried a six shooter. Only a rifle when out for game."

Blaine went into the saloon and Kilkenny walked out to his horse and swung into the saddle. He would be better off at home minding his own business, but if trouble was coming to the KR and to Nita, he wanted to know it.

He took the east road out of town and lifted the buckskin into a space-eating canter. When he found a trail leading off south, he took it, and finally found a crude sign painted with the one word *Carpenter's* and an arrow. He followed along into the late dusk, and came up to the house, riding carefully.

A man's voice called out. "Hold it, stranger! Don't come no further!"

Kilkenny drew up and replied, "I'm friendly, Carpenter. Friendly, and curious."

"Don't get you."

"Had any visitors lately?"

"What's that to you?"

"Like I said, I'm curious. I'd sort of like to talk a little."

"I've got nothin' to say. Nothin' at all. And," he added dryly, "I never seen you before."

"I'm Trent. Just a loose-footed hombre who has a curious mind. I'm sort of wonderin' where a man would put ten or fifteen thousand head of cattle in this country without crowdin' a lot of other folks."

There was a silence and then low conversation within the house. Finally, Carpenter spoke again. "Get down and come in, but don't try nothin' fancy. We folks got faith in shotguns."

Kilkenny swung down and trailing the reins, walked up to the house, keeping his hands wide. A bar was removed from the door and he entered.

Carpenter was a solid looking citizen, and his wife had the firm, quiet face of a woman who knew how to build a home and had courage enough to build it anywhere. Carpenter on his side measured the tall man in the black jeans and gray shirt with a thoughtful eye. "What's on your mind?" he said at last.

"Why, nothin' much." Kilkenny dropped astride a chair. "Heard Carson got killed an' I was wonderin' whether you'd had visitors."

"I had 'em, all right." Carpenter told his story briefly and without decoration. "I reckon," he finished, "it was only my woman saved me, an' her only because they didn't like the looks o' the shotgun. Maybe," he added, "because they'd already had trouble with Carson."

Kilkenny told them what he knew of Tetlow and the thousands of cattle they were bringing over the trail, and he hinted that he had an interest, purely personal, in the KR. Carpenter chuckled and his wife smiled. "I reckon," he said, "it don't take no wizard to figure out why. That Nita Riordan is a wonderful girl."

"Don't mention me to them," Kilkenny requested, "that will come in good time. But I know Brigo an' you can count on him to stick. You should have a talk with her."

"Good advice," Carpenter agreed. "Talkin' with old Dan an' some others wouldn't be a bad idea, either."

Kilkenny returned to his horse and drew it back into the trees. For several minutes he watched and listened with care natural to him after the years of his life. Then he mounted and took another route homeward. It was customary for him to do that, also. It could have been merest chance that the trail he took skirted the holdings of the KR and neared the house at one place.

He drew up when he saw the lights and he sat there a long time, looking at them. There, where those lights glowed softly in the evening, was the only girl he had ever loved. There, no more than two hundred yards away, with all her warmth, her beauty, her tenderness and her humor. A girl to walk beside a man, and walk with him, not behind him. He rolled a smoke and lighted up, and spoke softly to Buck. "She's there, Buck, old boy, there in that house. Remember her, Buck? Remember how she looked the first time we saw her? Remember the light in her eyes and the way her lips parted a little? Remember her, Buck?"

The horse stirred under him, and he spoke to it softly, then rode on, and riding on, he did not look back. Had he looked back he would have seen a big man, broad and powerful, step from the darker shadows and stare after him. A man who carried a rifle, and who after a moment of waiting, lighted his own cigarette revealing a strongly handsome, yet savage face. And when he walked away with the cigarette cupped in his palm, his feet made no sound, but moved silently through the brush and grass, silently even over the gravel.

He walked up toward the house, and nearing it, saw another man seated in the black opening of the bunkhouse door. "It's me, Cain." The man's voice was low, a soft, fluid tone. "*He* was out there tonight, Cain."

Cain Brockman came to his feet, a huge man, bulking an easy two forty in jeans and a hickory shirt. Twin guns were belted to his hips. "You mean . . . *Kilkenny?*"

"Si, amigo." Jaime Brigo drew deep on his cupped cigarette. "And I am glad."

"Are you going to tell *her?*"

Brigo shrugged. "Who knows? I have not thought. Maybe he does not wish it."

"Yeah, although he's crazy not to. What man in his right mind would run away from such a woman as that?"

Brigo did not answer, taking another deep drag on the cigarette and then crushing it out in the earth at his feet. "Perhaps, amigo, he does well. Who knows when such a man may die? He thinks of that."

"Anybody who kills him," Cain said gruffly, "will have to shoot him in the back! Nobody ever lived could drag a gun like him."

"They shot Wild Bill so. Have you forgotten? Be sure that *he* has not. But I am glad he is here, for there will be trouble with the Forty."

Brockman agreed to that. "When wasn't there trouble with the Tetlows? Don't I know? I was in Uvalde when they started that fight with the McCann outfit."

He sat down again, then he wondered aloud, "Where's he livin'? Suppose he's got him a place?"

Brigo did not reply, and Brockman turned to repeat the question and saw the big Yaqui was gone. He had slipped away with no more sound than a ghost.

Jaime Brigo tapped softly on the door of the ranch house and he heard the reply. Opening the door, he stepped in, a huge man, big-chested and yet moving like a cat.

Nita Riordan smiled quickly, a tall girl with long green eyes and very black lashes. "Come in, Jaime! It's good to see you. What has been happening?"

Briefly, the big Yaqui explained to her about the shooting of Carson and the threatening of Carpenter, of which he had heard almost at once. They had talked of this before, and he had been working for the family long before her father's death and knew how this girl felt about such things. He told her what he had been able to find out about the Tetlows and how they had come into the country with their immense herds, many wagons, and Tetlow's four sons—of whom but three were left.

"The other?"

"He was killed at Clifton's." Brigo hesitated and Nita looked up quickly, her face suddenly white.

"Jaime! Was it . . . was it *Lance?*"

The Yaqui shrugged. "I do not know, señorita. It was a tall man in black. He was riding through. It was young Tetlow who began it. He forced the fight on the other man, who was already wounded."

"Do you think we'll ever see him again, Jaime?"

Brigo hesitated, tempted to tell her of what he had seen this night, yet he was torn between two loyalties, that to his employer and friend, and that to the man she loved—who was also his friend. And whom he understood as few men could. "I think—yes, I think so," he said at last. "He will come back one day, when you need him he will come."

"You sound so sure."

"And you?" Jaime asked shrewdly. "Are you not sure?"

"Yes, I guess I am." She got up quickly. "Jaime, is Cain out there on watch? If he is, why don't you have him come in? I'll make some coffee for both of you. Maria has gone to bed."

Brigo nodded and turned to the door. He was gone almost without a sound. Nita walked through the short hallway to the kitchen. Had she been imagining it, or had Jaime seemed *too* sure? Had he seen Kilkenny? She shook her head, dismissing the thought. No, he would not be here, of all places. Yet deep within her she knew it was not only possible but probable, for Kilkenny moved in the loneliest places, and the newest countries, and this one was new.

Then her mind turned to the threat implied by the coming of Tetlow. Accustomed to border warring, she understood what that threat meant as well as any cowhand or rancher in the country. She knew much of men such as he, and knew that he must have not a little land, not a little range, but lots of it. All there was here would not be too much. Realistic as she was, she also foresaw the influence the buying power would have on the businessmen of Horsehead. They would be reluctant to make any move that would in any way displease so big a potential customer, never foreseeing what he could mean to them with his grasping and autocratic way.

What should she do? That alone she did not know. Within a few days she would be faced with the problem and it was not one that pleased her. Better able to resist than the others, because she not only had made friends in town but she had several very able men who were not only excellent hands but who were gun handlers as well. As far as Cain Brockman and Brigo were concerned, she knew that with the possible exception of Havalik the Forty outfit had nobody who could equal them, let alone top them. The Forty had many more, but remembering the lessons learned from her own experiences and those learned from Kilkenny, she had built here with the realization that a time might come when the place would have to be defended, and it could be. Moreover, behind her was the towering wall of Comb Ridge, practically shutting off all advance from that direction.

The four hands that she now employed other than Brigo, who acted as foreman, were all good men and personally known to her. Cain Brockman was not only a good fighting man and cunning, but he was loyal to the death. It was strange the influence that Kilkenny had had upon the former outlaw. That Brockman had been a killer she knew. How many men lay behind him she did not know, but it was generally estimated that he had killed over a dozen before meeting Kilkenny.

Pacing the floor nervously, she waited for them to come in, and when the door opened, she looked up smiling. Cain came in first, a burly, clumsy-looking man with huge fists, a thick, muscular neck and a hairy chest visible through his opened shirt. His nose had been flattened and he had heavy cheekbones and a heavy jaw, one of the toughest-looking men she had ever seen.

"Evenin', ma'am," he said, "sure is nice o' you to have us in for coffee. You make the best coffee I ever did drink."

"Thanks, Cain. Are the rest of the boys asleep?"

"Yeah, they had a hard day of it. That Comb Ridge sure is a help though. Like a fence, only it never needs to be fixed. No post holes to dig. Reckon yuh got about a thousand head scattered between Westwater an' Comb."

"In the morning, Jaime," Nita Riordan turned suddenly to the Yaqui, "have my horse saddled. I'm riding into town."

"Si." Jaime Brigo dropped into a chair wondering if the tall rider from the shadow of the trees would be in town. Cain had asked a good question: where was he living? It would be wise to find out in case they needed him.

"Also," she added, "I want none of the men riding the range alone from now on. I want them to ride two by two, and keep their eyes open. If they have killed one man, they will not hesitate to kill others. However, I'm going to see Leal Macy."

Dawn broke over the hills and Kilkenny rolled out of his bed in the Westwater Hotel and began to dress. He had been rising at daybreak for so long that he could no longer sleep even if he wanted to. This morning he was anxious to be up and around. He wanted to judge the town's reaction to the killing of Carson.

He went down the stairs and turned into the dining room. Doc Blaine was the only man there, but a few minutes later the young man he had spotted as Tetlow came into the room. He glanced at Doc and then at Kilkenny with friendly, questioning eyes. Neither appeared to notice him, and flushing, he seated himself alone.

The waitress came in and took their orders and Blaine ate in silence. "Trouble?" Kilkenny asked at last.

"Usual. Root's wife is ailing. She's worked all her life to help her husband build a home and she's killing herself. She needs a rest more than anything else. She don't want me to examine her, but I'm going to. Nice family. Poor," he added, "but energetic. The kind of people who do half the work of the world but never succeed in profiting from it. Stubborn, sincere, hard-working, but not acquisitive."

"You find them all over the West," Kilkenny said. He grinned suddenly. "Maybe I'm one of them."

Blaine looked up briefly, looking right into Kilkenny's eyes directly and with faint humor. "You're a Western type, as familiar as they are," he said, "but different."

"You've got me pegged?"

"Of course. You're a cut above the average of your type, but still one of them. You're not even strictly a Western product. Your type has drifted up and down the world since it began. The lone hunter, the man on the prowl, the fighter for lost causes, the man who understands weapons better than women and understands women quite well. Yes, I know your type. They sailed with Drake, they built the Hudson Bay Company. They were the backbone of the free companies of the Middle Ages."

"You're flattering."

"Am I?" Blaine looked up quickly. "Well, it depends on how you take it. Flattering, perhaps, but not reassuring. Your type fights the wars of the world and gets nothing from it but a lonely grave somewhere and the memory in the minds of a few men who die and then there is nothing."

Kilkenny laughed softly, his green eyes lighting up. "Yes, maybe you're right." As the doctor got to his feet, he added, "Give my regards to the Roots. Tell them a man named Trent will call on them some day."

When Blaine had gone, Kilkenny turned to his meal with interest and a hunger he had not realized he possessed. He was aware of the presence of Ben Tetlow but he said nothing and made no move to speak. The door opened and another man entered. Both looked up. This was a tall, fine appearing man with a trimmed gray mustache, gray hair and a fine, aristocratic face and the bearing to match. "Good morning, gentlemen," he said. "I don't believe we've met. I'm Robert Early."

"Trent, here."

The lawyer looked at him keenly. "Heard about you. My niece tells me you gave her quite a shock at Clifton's."

Ben Tetlow was scarcely listening, but at that name he stiffened. Kilkenny threw him a quick glance, but Ben Tetlow did not look up. Sensing something wrong, Early glanced quickly from one to the other, puzzled by their reaction.

Tetlow was thinking swiftly. Yesterday Laurie Webster, this man's niece, had mentioned seeing Trent kill a man. Now Early said it had happened at Clifton's. Of course, other men had been killed there, but this could only mean one man. Trent had killed his brother!

Ben glanced sharply around, staring at this man. He recalled what they had said. The flashing draw, the one shot, the gun only half-drawn from his brother's holster. And his brother had been considered fast, had bragged that he was faster than Billy the Kid.

"Your niece is a very lovely girl," Kilkenny was saying, "and I'm truly sorry for what happened. One can't always choose the course of one's actions. I wanted no trouble."

"So I heard." Early ordered and looked back at him. "Staying with us?"

"Yes." Kilkenny was acutely aware of the presence of Tetlow. Inwardly he was wondering what Ben's course of action would be. This was the only Tetlow he had actually talked to except for the dead brother, but he seemed agreeable and anxious to be friendly. "Yes, I like it here and I think I'll stay."

He finished his meal and got to his feet. Outside the street was crowded with Tetlow riders. A dozen horses were tied in front of the sheriff's office and he glanced over that way. What had Macy done about the death of Carson?

He strolled across the street, walking around a knot of armed men. They were typical cowhands in dress, but there was that about them that told him they were something more. He knew the breed. These were fighting men, drawing warriors' wages.

Behind his desk stood Leal Macy. The jailer lounged in the corner. Macy was speaking, and the man to whom he talked was Havalik. Beside the latter was Phin Tetlow.

"The inquest," Macy said sternly, "will be at ten o'clock. You be there, Havalik. We'll get this matter settled right now."

Havalik shrugged. "Oh, all right, but it's a lot of fuss over nothin'. The hombre asked for it."

"That will be established at the inquest," Macy replied coolly.

"Supposin'," Havalik jeered, "that you decide I'm guilty. What happens then?"

"You'll be arrested, put in jail and held for trial," Macy replied quietly.

Havalik laughed, a laugh echoed by several of the Forty riders. "Arrest *me?*" he laughed. "Why, you ain't man enough to arrest me in the first place, an' no Forty hand ever did a day in jail in the second place. The outfit would pull this jail down around your ears."

"They might," Macy replied, "but if they did the law would hunt down every man jack of them. It may have escaped your notice, Havalik, but times are changing. You fellows are on short notice everywhere now. The day when killing could go unpunished in the West is over."

"Yeah?" Havalik laughed again. "That's right interestin' to know. I sure would admire to see you ride onto any range held by the Forty to take one o' their men."

Leal Macy was not cowed. Calmly, he replied, "If that becomes necessary, that is exactly what I shall do. We will hold the inquest in the Diamond Palace at ten. Be there." Deliberately, he turned his back and walked into the jail behind the desk. The others turned and trooped out and there was a rush for the Pinenut Saloon. Kilkenny stood out of the way and watched them go, and then he stepped into the office. Macy reappeared from the jail, his face cold.

He nodded to Kilkenny. "That bunch is riding for a fall," he said.

"Uh-huh." Kilkenny dropped in the chair in which he had sat on the previous day. "How much help can you get here in town?"

Macy looked at him quickly, then he smiled without humor. "Very little, I'm afraid. A few good men. The rest will be looking at the buttered side of their bread."

"What I figured." Kilkenny ran his fingers through his hair and looked down at his boots. "I like a man with nerve, Macy. Count me in if you need help."

Macy studied him carefully. "All right," he replied, "but no obligations, understand? Wherever my duty takes me, I'll go."

"Sure." Kilkenny got to his feet. "I'm asking no favors nor giving any. This fight if it comes will be everybody's fight, only most of them won't know it until it's too late."

Leal Macy nodded shortly and as Kilkenny reached the door, Macy glanced up. "Thanks, Trent. I appreciate this."

"Sure." Kilkenny stepped out into the street. If there was going to be trouble there was little sense in delaying action and allowing the Tetlows to get too firmly situated. He wanted no trouble, but he knew now there would be no avoiding it. If Ben had been the boss—that fellow could be talked to. Maybe it would be worth attempting.

Three men were standing in front of the stage station. They were the same men he had seen in the hotel dining room. The big man with the lumbering gait was staring at him truculently. Suddenly, he yelled, "Hey, you!"

Kilkenny ignored him and the man yelled again, then wheeled and started for Kilkenny, who came along and stepped up on the walk in front of the Westwater. There the big man reached him. "When I call, yuh stop!" he bellowed, thrusting his face at Kilkenny.

Suddenly, Lance Kilkenny was coldly, bitterly furious. The attitude of the man, his bullying voice, the attitude of the Forty outfit toward the sheriff, all of it had culminated in this. His right hand jerked up, not in a closed fist, but striking up with the butt of his palm. The movement was so swift the big man had no chance to avoid it and the hard butt of that palm smashed under his jaw, slamming his head back on his neck. The man tottered, and Kilkenny stepped in and struck him a slashing blow across the side of the face with the edge of his palm. The blow laid the man's cheek open for four inches, showering him with blood. Then Kilkenny looked up, facing the other two men.

The man with the white eyes and the gun tucked in his waistband and the man with the missing finger and scarred face. Both stared down at the big fellow on the ground and then looked at Kilkenny unbelieving. "Never even closed his fist!" somebody said from the gathering crowd.

"This gent's hunting trouble, Grat," the scar-faced man said softly. "He's askin' for it."

"Then we'll give it to him, Red." Grat started to move, but he was too late. Kilkenny had seen the situation developing and preferred it to be settled with fists rather than guns. Infinitely more experienced at this sort of thing than the average cowhand, he struck swiftly. The blow caught Grat high on the face, and as his hands came up to protect his face, he whipped an underhand blow to the wind. Grat's knee caved and he pitched forward into the cracking left hook that Kilkenny had ready for him.

When he stepped in to meet Grat he had turned in such a way as to put Grat between himself and Red. It gave him just time enough to put Grat out of the running, and as Red rushed him, Kilkenny vaulted over the hitch rail into the street. Red brought up short and in the split second of hesitation, Kilkenny grabbed his outstretched arm and threw his back under him, jerking him over the rail and off his back with a flying mare. Stunned, Red stared up, gasping for breath at the man who stood over him.

"I'm not hunting trouble," Kilkenny said, "but it's time somebody showed you where to head in. If you've picked me for the job, I'm the man who can do it."

Jared Tetlow shoved through the crowd, his face flushed and angry. "Here! What goes on here?"

Kilkenny turned sharply at the authority in the voice. His head dropped a little, his hands went wide. "Tetlow!" His voice rang in the narrow street. "You came into this country hunting trouble and you brought a bunch of no-good trouble-hunters with you! These hands of yours jumped me!"

A devil was driving him now and he was cold with fury. He stepped toward the older man, his hands ready to his guns. He felt it building inside him but was helpless to stop it. He was berserk with fury and ready for anything, heedless of anything. He could not have stopped had he faced the whole Forty outfit.

"Take 'em and get out of the country! Move 'em out! You've come looking for trouble and here it is! And if you don't like what I say—*fill your hand!*"

Jared Tetlow was appalled. Accustomed to command, surrounded by tough gunhands who protected him from every danger, it had been years since he had personally faced a gun. In company with his men he faced up to them readily, but now, suddenly, he felt lost, alone. He fought for words and none would come. Suddenly, he knew with cold certainty that if he reached for his gun he would die.

Never had he been so aware of the imminence of death. This man would kill him. That realization shook him to the depths of his being. Normally courageous, he had been so protected in the past years that now, naked and alone, he was helpless to move.

Slowly, Kilkenny relaxed. "So that's how it is?" he said contemptuously. "Nerve enough to order a man killed but not nerve enough to face it yourself!"

Deliberately, he turned his back and walked across the street and into the hotel, leaving behind him a blanket of silence.

Jared Tetlow stared around him as if coming out of a trance. Realization came to him. He had been challenged, had been dared to draw and he had made no move. There were thinly veiled smiles on some of the faces, worry on others. Around him the crowd was melting away.

His definite, known world seemed suddenly shaky. He had grown to manhood in a family that fought as a unit. He had trained his sons and his riders the same way. It was always the Forty against everything and everybody, but one man had thrown a challenge into their teeth and he himself had backed down.

Grat got to his feet, sullenly beating the dust from his clothing. The wide cut on Jess Baker's face seeped blood. Red, at the hitch rail, was being violently sick. Tetlow glanced around and saw Ben standing in front of the harness shop. His emptiness filled with fury. "You!" he roared. "Where were you? Why didn't you do something?"

"What could I do? If I had made a move he would have killed you—just like he killed Bud."

Jared Tetlow went stiff with shock. "That . . . it was . . . *he* killed Bud?"

"That's the man," Ben said quietly, "and if anyone had made a wrong move he would have killed you!"

FOUR

Kilkenny entered the hotel to find Leal Macy waiting for him. The sheriff seemed unusually quiet. "That took nerve," he commented, "what if he had tried it?"

"He wouldn't," Kilkenny said. "He's a cinch killer. I saw them work against Lott the other day."

"But he might have."

"Yes, I thought he would, to be honest. Or maybe I just didn't think. Their kind get in my craw."

"Mine, too. But you'd better get out of town for a few days at least. They'll never rest now until they get you."

"What about the hearing?"

"We'll have it." Macy spoke flatly. "We'll have it and we'll see what a local jury does. The fact is, your stand here in the street may make all the difference. They may not hesitate to bring in a bill against them. Or against Havalik."

"You'll have a fight if you try to arrest him."

"Then I'll have it." Macy was grim and quiet. "There are a few good men in town. Early is one of them, Doc Blaine is another."

"Doc?" Kilkenny was surprised.

Macy nodded. "Oddly enough, he's a fighter. Plenty of sand and a fine rifle shot."

"You can count on Dolan."

"Dolan?" Macy stared, half angry. "You think I'd call on him for help?"

"Why not? It doesn't look to me like you have much choice. I'd say call on him. Dolan," he added, "is a former Army man. He

42

was a soldier for quite some years. Despite the fact that he's on the edge of the law now, such a man is deeply marked with his former experience, and against mob action. Dolan will stand hitched, and keep his boys so. Also, he considers the Forty as fair game."

Macy considered that. It went against the grain to ask help or even accept offered help from a man of Dolan's stamp, yet Macy had been a soldier himself, and he knew how deeply the years of training were imbedded in a man's nature. And Dolan had not been a citizen soldier, but a Regular Army man, a sergeant of long experience, accustomed to order and discipline. He still bore the mark of it in his neat dress, his square shoulders and his walk, and the sharpness of his actions. It was possible that Kilkenny was right.

"I'll stay if you want," Kilkenny volunteered. He admired the stand this man was taking. It was such men whom the West needed if ever there was to be peace and order.

"No, you'd only be another bone of contention. They'll be out to get you now, and your presence might make all the difference. You better leave town—and watch your back trail."

"That," Kilkenny said wryly, "is something I always do."

When he was gone, Leal Macy looked after him, a faint frown between his eyes. He had not quite decided what to think about this man. Kilkenny talked right and sized up as all man, yet out there in the street he had been a man driven by the urge to kill, a man literally aching for the fight he expected. That could be a bad thing unless regulated by a stern will. Macy turned that last thought over in his mind, and shook his head. He was not sure.

Kilkenny got his horse and started out of town. The streets were deserted now, but he rode west, his horse's hoofs pounding briefly on the bridge. In front of Dolan's he drew up and called. Dolan came to the door, his hands thrust in his coat pockets, a cigar clamped in his teeth. Kilkenny had an urge to shout "Attention!" but stifled it. He had no doubt Dolan would snap to, and might enjoy it. No matter which side of the law this man now stood upon, he would stand under fire, a cool disciplined mind and hand.

"Leaving town," Kilkenny commented. "Macy may need help. I told him he could count on you."

Dolan was startled. He took the cigar from his teeth and spat, then stared at the end of it before he looked up. "What the devil inspired that?"

"I know the breed, Dolan." He turned his horse and rode off down the street.

Dolan swore, threw his cigar into the street, then walked into the club and dropped into the chair behind his desk. Without being aware of it he lighted a fresh cigar and stared into the blue smoke of it.

He picked up a week-old San Francisco paper and straightened it with a jerk that almost tore it. Then he looked up at a square-built man who sat against the wall. "Pete, round up Clyde and Shorty. Maybe two or three others who'll stand hitched. We're going to that inquest. We," he added, "are going to side the sheriff."

"The sheriff?" Pete blinked.

"Yes." Dolan had never explained his actions before. "We've a choice. If they bust Macy we'll have to fight the Forty alone. We want to keep Macy in action."

"That makes sense. The Forty stacks up to be mighty mean."

West of town Kilkenny took a trail into some scattered junipers. The background was desert and sandrock, dotted with greasewood. Against such a background his horse would merge into the landscape. From long practice he avoided metal on his clothing or horse. No man would wear glittering ornaments who was not a braggart or a fool. A chance reflection on a bright buckle or spangle had guided more than one bullet.

He worked to leave little trail, then emerged on a vast tableland and, swinging at right angles, rode east. He bedded down for the night on high ground among some rocks where he could overlook miles of country.

Just before dusk he saw two groups of men riding trails out of town, five in each group, at a rough guess. When it was completely dark he rolled in his blankets and was soon asleep.

At the camp of the Forty all was silent. Men ate quietly and slipped away to their bedrolls. All avoided the eyes of Jared Tetlow. Deeply shaken, the old man stared long into the fire.

The realization of failure lay heavy upon him but he had been too long in command not to know what he must do now. Anything less than prompt action would end his hold upon the men who followed him, and he knew that reprisal must be swift, sure, and bitter. They had always known he was not a gunman, but they also knew that whoever this man Trent was, he was gunslick. Now that Ben's account of how he knew that Trent was the man who killed Bud was around camp, all knew that Trent was a gunfighter.

Under the circumstances they would not blame him, but if he held back now they would lose faith in his courage. Moreover, the inquest on this day had not gone well. He had planned to strike there, to carry it off with a high hand and deny the right of Macy or anyone to question his actions. Then the man Dolan had arrived with several hardcase riders, all armed. They had said nothing, but Dolan was obviously with the sheriff, which was surprising.

Moreover, despite the number of businessmen who had remained away, Bob Early had been there, and Doc Blaine as well, and their position had left no doubt. Autocratic as he might be, there was that something deep within Tetlow that made him respect the authority of leading citizens. They were his kind of men, he felt, and their prestige counted for more than the threat of Dolan's guns.

Early himself had conducted the inquest. It had been sharp and direct. There were no witnesses except those for Havalik, but several witnesses were put on the stand who testified that Carson had never carried a gun. The possibility that he might have had one on that day remained and there was insufficient evidence to warrant holding Dee Havalik. Nevertheless, the weight of public opinion had made itself felt, and Tetlow was irritated by it.

Viewing the matter from the distance, he regretted the shooting of Carson not one whit. He regretted only that they had hesitated to ride roughshod over Carpenter, Marable, and the lot of them. There was little that public opinion or anyone could do against the accomplished fact.

The first thing had been to find Kilkenny and wipe him out, and realizing that at once, two groups of Forty riders had been sent out to track him down and kill him. Moreover, Tetlow had been shrewd enough to let it be known that Kilkenny, or Trent as he knew him, had killed his son at Clifton's.

So far the riders sent after him had not been heard from, but they were covering all trails and should find him without trouble. That they would kill on sight, or hang him if they caught him alive, had been their orders as well as their conviction. Bud had been the most popular of his sons with the rougher element.

Ben walked up to the fire and seated himself close to his father. For awhile he smoked in silence. "Dad, let's drive on west. Let's leave this place."

When there was no answer, he steeled himself to go on. It took courage, for Ben Tetlow knew how his father hated weakness, and he also knew what must be going through his father's mind tonight after the facing down he had taken in the streets of Horsehead.

"We're buckin' a stacked deck. There isn't enough range here unless we take it all, and if we start fighting women and other settlers, we're out of luck. They'll band together against us."

"If you ain't got the guts for it, Ben," Tetlow replied stiffly, "get out!"

"No," Ben said quietly, "I'm staying. You're my father and this is our outfit. I'm stickin' even if I think you're wrong, and I do think you are. That's the trouble, Dad, you're committing others to your policy. If you go down you take a lot of men down with you. Some of them mighty good men."

"Leave him alone," Phin spoke from the darkness. "Like he says, if you don't like it, get out while the gettin's good."

Ben was silent, despair mounting in him. He had always entertained doubts of this business of riding roughshod over others, of insisting that their larger herd held inherent rights over all smaller herds and less powerful outfits. Yet there was no give in Leal Macy. The man would stand his ground until death, and for one, Ben was sure that Macy held the right stand.

Dolan was another. He knew how surprised he had been when Dolan showed, and how surprised his father had been. They had heard he was a leader or directing brain behind rustling and rustlers. They heard his place was a resort of the hardcase element, but the way the man stood and his looks belied that. Dolan was a fitting partner for Macy, and the two made a dangerous combination.

Ben had not thought much about Kilkenny. The fact that the man had killed his brother remained in his mind and for that reason he felt he should hate him, yet he could not bring himself to do so. He had the story from one of the older hands who had seen it all, and Bud had deliberately picked the fight, forced it when the man was ready to let it pass. And there had been no quarrel to precede it. Moreover, he felt drawn to the tall, quiet man with the brown face and the easy smile. He was, he appeared, a friendly man.

And then today in the street when he had called Ben's father, he had seen a different personality. In a land where fighting men were the rule rather than the exception, where courage was admired and strength and agility to be looked up to, Kilkenny was a commanding figure. The man had stepped out into that street heedless of all the Forty riders and their threat of power. He had slashed his way through three of them with his bare hands and then faced down his father in such a way as Ben had never seen a man faced. Ben had the courage of his convictions and his convictions were strong enough, but he saw something indomitable in that single-handed stand against the whole Forty outfit.

He had seen something else that none of the others seemed to see. It had not been superior strength that won that fight of one against three. Nor had it even been the violence, shocking in itself, of his onslaught. It had been superior skill and strategy. Kilkenny had never wasted a move. He had known exactly what to do and how to do it. Such skill was no accident. This man was a trained, experienced fighting man.

Jared Tetlow got to his feet. "Phin?" he questioned his son's wakefulness. At the grunted reply, he said, "Carpenter's got range enough for maybe six hundred head. We've got six thousand here now and more comin'. Crowd that range with four thousand head come daylight. Understand? We'll show this town how a Tetlow fights!"

Ben stared at the cold line of his father's jaw. There was no yielding there. Quietly he retreated to his blankets where he lay long awake.

*   *   *

At daylight the cattle were started. Deliberately, they hazed the cattle onto Carpenter's range while the rancher stood helplessly watching from beside his wife. At this rate within a few days they would have him ruined; what grass they had not eaten would be trampled underfoot.

Sitting his big chestnut, Tetlow watched grimly. Then he called to Ben. "You!" he said. "You've no stomach for this, so ride back down the trail an' tell them to push those cattle through fast! We'll show 'em who's going to run this here range!"

Havalik rode up beside him, his small face tight-lipped with satisfaction.

"When those herds get here, an' they should make it by the day after tomorrow, push them on the KR range," he said, "we'll have them out of there within the week!"

Riding east, Ben stared grimly at the skyline. Trust his father to think of the one way he could beat them. Nobody had legal authority to make him move his cattle. This was open range, and belonged to the government. No laws regulated it as yet, and even if they had, they could not operate fast enough to save these smaller men. His father could stand a loss if need be, these men could not. Even if his father was forced to move—which he would not be—the range would be ruined for most of the season. The grass would come back, but much of it would be so trampled and overgrazed that the range would be destroyed or injured. His father, with his great holdings and armed riders, could move on or take a loss. These small ranchers could not. Jared Tetlow would ride to power and victory behind a wall of thousands of cattle.

Carpenter stared gloomily at the thousands of cattle on his range. Desperate fury consumed him and his big fists knotted and balled iron hard. He wanted to fight, to strike out at something, at anything. But what could he do?

"We'd better leave the place," his wife said quietly. "Let's go up to the KR like that man said. Let's go up there and get Marable an' the Roots. Together maybe we can do something."

"I'll be damned if I will!" Carpenter flared. "Leave my place? Be driven off what's rightfully mine? I will not!"

* * *

The story of the cattle drive reached the KR with the story of the challenge to Tetlow issued in the streets of Horsehead. It was no garbled account, but was given concisely and definitely by Doc Blaine over lunch at the ranch house. Aside from Nita, only Jaime Brigo was there.

Blaine's story started casually enough. "Lots of excitement in town. Fellow whipped three of the Forty hands in less than that many minutes and then called old Jared Tetlow to his face. Dared him at point blank range. I never saw such a thing."

Brigo's eyes were steady on Blaine's face. The big Yaqui sensed what was coming.

Nita called Maria to pour some coffee. "He moved cattle on the Carpenter place this morning. He'll ruin the man."

"That seems to be the idea," Blaine agreed. "Have you thought about yourself?"

"Of course. He can't run as many cattle as he wants without my place." Doc Blaine watched her as she talked. She seemed scarcely more than a girl, yet there was an assurance about her that puzzled him. He knew nothing of her beyond the fact that she had bought out a previous rancher for cash, had built here a ranch home that was far superior in every way to anything around, and she lived in the saddle, worked cattle herself and yet supervised a home that was the most perfect thing he had seen this side of a French chateau. "If he tries that, he will have trouble."

"He has a lot of men."

"And I have Jaime. And Cain Brockman and some others."

"Is Brockman as tough as he looks?"

"Far tougher. I only knew one man who could handle him. Jaime might. I don't know."

"That fellow who faced down Tetlow," Blaine mused, "he's a drifting cowhand, and I think a gunfighter. There are rumors around that he was the man who killed young Bud Tetlow, but he seems like a good man. Why don't you hire him?"

"I don't think we'll need anybody else," Nita smiled, "but thanks just the same."

"You'd better think it over," Blaine insisted, "this man Trent—"

Her head came up sharply. "Who? Who did you say?"

Doc Blaine was surprised. "Why, Trent. At least, that's the name he uses. You can't tell about names, especially with drifters. They might use any name."

Nita was looking accusingly at Brigo. "Is it . . .?" There was no need to repeat the question for she could see the answer in the Yaqui's eyes and her heart began to pound. Unable to control herself, she came quickly to her feet, then, not wanting them to see her face, she turned quickly and walked to the window. "You . . . how long have you known?"

"The night before last. He came by here, and stopped outside."

"You . . . you talked to him?"

"No. He did not see me. I don't think he saw me."

Blaine looked from one to the other. Too wise in the way of the world and women to be fooled, he could see that Nita Riordan was upset. This surprised and intrigued him, for he had never seen anything startle her before. She was annoyingly self-possessed, and Blaine had been puzzled and disturbed by that self-possession. It was something he was not accustomed to in women, and it disconcerted him.

"You know this man called Trent?"

"I . . . I don't know. I think perhaps I do. I . . . we knew a man once who used that name."

"What was his real name?"

She turned on him. "That, Doctor, is something he would have to tell you himself." Then she remembered what the doctor had been saying, that this man had faced down Tetlow. Yes, she told herself, her heart pounding, that would be like Lance. He could never stand tyranny of any kind, and he would not hesitate because of numbers.

Lance . . .!

The thought of him disturbed her, and she stood staring out the window, remembering every line of his face. The way he smiled, the way the laugh wrinkles came faintly at the corners of his eyes, eyes long accustomed to squinting against desert suns. She remembered the quick way he walked, the strong brown hands, the way his green eyes could grow cold—although they had never grown cold when they looked at her.

She remembered that first day down in the Live Oak country, the day she had first seen him. She had looked across that room at him and suddenly they had seemed alone, as if only they remained in life and nothing else could or did exist. She had looked into his eyes and known this man wanted her, and had known that she wanted him, and they were right for each other and nothing else in the world would ever matter but him.

And now he was here again, close to her. He had been outside in the darkness, nearby. Had he known she was there? Had he been thinking of her? What had been his thoughts as he stood out there in the shadows, watching the lights? What time had it been? Had she been reading? Or getting ready for bed? Or already with her head upon the pillow?

"Jaime," she turned swiftly, "I want to see him."

The Yaqui looked at her and nodded. "Si, but to find him, who knows how? He is like the wind, and he leaves no trail."

"Think, Jaime! Where would he be? Remember what he said? That you did not follow a trail on the ground unless you could also trail with the mind? You have to think as the man you follow thinks, then you know where to go. You know him, Jaime. Where would he be?"

The big Yaqui shrugged, but he was thinking. That was the way, of course. To follow him with the mind. It was like the deer—once you knew where he watered it was not hard to find where he slept and where he fed. It was the same with all game, and with men. They established patterns. Kilkenny had said that, and he had never forgotten, for Kilkenny could follow a trail where even an Apache would fail.

But to follow the trail of Lance Kilkenny was something else again, for he was one who knew how to think, and knowing that he followed men by their patterns of thought as well as by their tracks upon the sand, he would think in different ways at different times. That, too, he had told Brigo.

One possibility there was. He would want a place that was far off and lonely, difficult to find and easy to defend, a place where he might stand off his enemies if need be. Especially would he want such a place with the Tetlows to consider.

"I think—maybe I could find him," he ventured. "I could try, but to be away from here now? It is not good."

"Find him!" Nita insisted. "Tell him I must see him."

"Perhaps there is another way," Blaine ventured. "Wait until he comes back into town. He will come, you know, and I know from what Leal Macy said that he has offered to back him if he needs help. Dolan knows him also." Blaine scowled thoughtfully. "Dolan might even know where he is. He would know if anybody does."

"Jaime. Ride to town with the doctor. Find out if Dolan does know."

Despite her anxiety it almost frightened her to think of seeing him again. She understood well enough his motives for leaving her as he had, and respected him for it even while she regretted it. That she was quite prepared to accept him despite what might happen he well knew. Yet the thought of seeing him again and the chance of losing him again frightened her. After his disappearance she had adjusted herself only after a long time, and doubted if she could go through it again.

Her childhood training, her father, all her background conditioned her to love for one man only. Moreover, there was something inwardly fastidious about her that avoided the thought of any other man but this one.

"Let me go to Dolan," Blaine suggested. "I know him. I'll explain, and then you'll have Brigo if trouble starts."

Brigo waited, liking this idea better. He had cared for Nita since she was a child and resented the thought of leaving her at such a time. Kilkenny was the only man who came near her of whom he approved. More than fifty years of age, the Yaqui possessed the strength of a gorilla, the devotion of a dog, and the cunning of a wolf.

"All right," Nita decided. "Tell him I need to see him."

Doc Blaine got up from the table. Curiously he wondered how she had met the man who called himself Trent. Obviously the man had used the name before, but who was he?

As he started back toward town in his buckboard he could see cattle darkening the range where once Carpenter's few cattle had grazed. How could a woman with so few hands hope to stand against Tetlow's vast herds? There was no way to fight masses of cattle, for now Jared Tetlow had found the method that seemingly could not be stopped. He himself need attack nobody, for those cattle, bunched upon range too small to feed them, would break any man.

Nearing Whiskers Draw a man got up from the rocks. He had a field glass and a rifle. It was Cain Brockman.

"Howdy," he grinned, slouching down to the trail. "Reckon we got a fight comin'."

"You may get help." Brockman had been with Nita a long time and might know. "Miss Riordan has asked me to get in touch with a man named Trent."

Excitement broke over Brockman's face. "You mean—" He broke off sharply. "Trent? Nobody I'd rather see right now."

Blaine had gone no more than two miles further when another movement stopped him. A woman, bloody and half her clothing torn, stumbled down the draw, then fell. She was struggling to rise as he reached her side. She was not a young woman and she was obviously exhausted as well as badly hurt. It was Mrs. Carpenter.

"My God! What's happened? Where's Free?"

"Dead." She was half dazed with grief and weariness. "Killed."

"Shot?"

"They stampeded cattle through the yard. He'd gone for water to the well. He broke for the house but he didn't get halfway before they ran him down."

"And you?"

"Tried to help him. Steer knocked me down. I . . . I was going for the sheriff."

He helped her into the buckboard and gave her a drink from his canteen. He wiped her face clean and gave her the best first aid treatment he could manage. "He was all I had," she mumbled, only half conscious. "Without him it ain't . . . it ain't . . ."

He put a hand on her shoulder. "Think what Free would have done. He was a brave, good man."

After that she sat quietly until they reached town. He turned off at the outskirts and drove to Bob Early's home.

Laurie Webster was watering flowers and when she saw the woman she hurried to help. Blaine explained quickly.

"Is Bob home?"

"He's at the Diamond. He was to meet Leal Macy there."

There would be action now. They would not take this. Yet even as the thought came to him, he began to doubt. Some would think only of the added profit they were making from the big, new outfit. They would remember the painfully few dollars spent by Carpenter and Carson, and would not allow themselves to think of what might happen when the Forty was in complete control.

There was Macy, however, and Bob Early. And there was Dolan and his men, perhaps a few others. His spirits sagged as he realized how few they were. Yet it had been always so. The many are afraid to act, hoping for the best until it is too late.

A dozen men sat at the table when he entered. Briefly, he explained. Macy leaned on the table, looking around at the faces of the others. "What did I tell you? Carson first, now Carpenter. Nobody is safe."

"We don't know what happened." Woolrich owned the Emporium. "We don't know Carpenter was run down a-purpose. We only got a hysterical woman's word for it."

Happy Jack Harrow of the Pinenut Saloon agreed. "My sentiments. Tetlow's bringing prosperity. My take's doubled since he came. This here's hard country. If a man ain't fit, he can't last."

"Who are we to fight a rancher's battles?" Savory agreed. "There's always been range wars. Far as that goes, what d'you suppose they'd do to the town if we started something? They'd wipe us out."

"So you'll stand by and see men murdered, robbed of their homes, and women driven into the desert?" Macy was disgusted. "Now we know the brand you wear, anyway."

"Easy with that, Sheriff." Savory's face was angry. "Because you're the law doesn't give you license to make free with your tongue. A bullet'll stop you soon as any man."

"Forget that," Early broke in. "Let's not fight among ourselves." He looked around. "I take it then that you're not in favor of taking action?"

"That's right," Savory said. Woolrich, Harrow, and a half dozen others nodded agreement.

Early turned to Macy. "Well, Leal, that shakes out the deck a little but the right cards can still win. I want you to deputize me."

"And me," Doc Blaine replied shortly.

A big man with a shock of black curly hair stepped up from the back of the room. His face was heavy-jawed and sullen. "I want you make me ziss deputy, too."

Pierre Ernleven was rarely seen away from his kitchen. He liked nothing so much as preparing food and seeing it eaten, and he took no part in the affairs of Horsehead. If he did not like a man's conversation or his attitude he would refuse to serve him. He was not above throwing a man bodily from the premises.

"Thanks, Pierre," Macy said. "There's no man I'd sooner have."

Ernleven looked around, his eyes bitter with contempt. "The rest of you don't come to my dining room. That goes for you, Harrow. Stay out."

Harrow got up, flushed and angry. "Cut your throats if you want. You don't know where your bread is buttered."

"That's probably right, Jack." Early spoke quietly. "We're thinking about a little word that has meant an awful lot to this country. A word called Justice. We're thinking of a country where there will be no feudal power, where no one man can control the destinies of others. It was little men who built this country, and little men who have been its backbone. You should read Jefferson, Harrow. Had you lived in '76 you'd have been a Tory."

"You call me a traitor?" Harrow's face went white.

"Examine your conduct," Early replied, "then judge for yourself. As for me," he got to his feet, "my Winchester needs oiling. Call on me, Leal, when you're ready." He turned away, then glanced back. "See you later, *gentlemen!*"

Harrow glared around him, then stamped out and slammed the door. Woolrich walked after him. He was gloomy. His wife would give him the devil for this. She thought anything Bob Early did was all right.

Macy smiled with wry humor. "There it is, Doctor. If you ever wanted a lost cause, you've got it."

Blaine refused to admit it. "The cause of right is never lost, Leal. I've often thought the biggest damn fool in the world could go down in history as a great man if he would just consistently vote for the greatest good of the greatest number.

"Take Andy Johnson. They hated him, called him a little man, reviled him, tried to impeach him to get the presidency in the hands of a man they could control. He voted as he believed right and acted as he believed. Now the reaction is setting in and most people believe he was right. This is a good cause, not a lost one."

"What about Dolan?"

"He's a seasoned fighter who'll take no back talk from any man. Also," Blaine smiled, "Dolan's Irish and the Irish have an inborn resentment against power and privilege. They imbibe it with their mother's milk."

They were silent, then Blaine looked up. "Who is this man Trent?"

Leal Macy hesitated. This question he had known would come. "I think," he said quietly, "that Trent is probably the fastest man with a gun in the West. I think Trent is Kilkenny."

"*Kilkenny?*" Blaine was shocked.

"I'm sure of it."

"Kilkenny . . ." Blaine muttered. "Kilkenny . . . here!"

FIVE

Dee Havalik had his order. They were to hunt down and kill Lance Kilkenny.

Macy's identification of Trent had swept the town. The dramatic scene when he challenged Tetlow and manhandled three of Tetlow's tough riders took on a new glow.

Dee Havalik heard the name with satisfaction. His gun speed was his great pride, and to hear another man named as fast aroused irritation in him. Small, slender-boned and pinched of face, he was a man compact of nervous energy and drive. Far from pleasant at any time, with a gun in his hand he became ice cold and passionless.

By choice three of those riding with him were the men Kilkenny had whipped in the street, and there were four others. One of these was an Apache trailer.

Within a few hours after they took the trail Kilkenny was aware of it. He studied them through his carefully shielded field glass. The make-up of the crew was evidence of its intention. The saddle packs and pack horses meant it was a hunt to the death. The issue was clearcut now. They must die or he would.

At once he struck north into the wildest and loneliest country. If they wanted a hunt, he would give it to them. This was the life he knew best, and there was no trick of white man or savage that he did not know. He rode north and the sun blazed down from a hot and copper sky. He struck out across the sage brush levels where no cattle grazed and where the rattler buzzed and the buzzard soared. He struck north and west and he left a trail they

57

could read without trouble, and deep in his chest something violent and frightening began to grow, the desire to turn on his pursuers and mow them down, to ride with the red lust of battle in him, ride right into their midst with guns blazing. But the time was not ripe for that, first he would show them what hell was like, he would show them what they had started!

The horizon danced and was lost in a haze of heat, the buzzards were the only spot of movement and the sun baked down upon the desert and the sand threw back the heat in his face like the top of a red hot stove. Their faces grew dusty, their throats parched, and riding on and on, he looked back upon his trail and saw the distant rising dust and chuckled. "Let 'em come!" he whispered. "Let 'em come!"

The surface of the desert broke into a maze of canyons, but he rode on. At waterholes he hesitated and waited, then pushed on when dark came. The days marched past and still he led them on, weaving among the canyons and taking them deeper and deeper into one of the most awful lands on the face of God's sometimes green earth. It was a land raw from the furnace of creation, a land without soil, rock shaped like flame and a sky that held no clouds but only a vast and blazing sun. Behind him his pursuers sweated and cursed, their lips parched and they nursed their canteens like mothers over a newborn child. They snarled at each other and grew vicious, and only Dee Havalik did not change except to grow thinner, leaner, and more vicious.

Tempers grew short and the men began to hate the land, the sun, each other. And then suddenly the chase changed, and it changed on one bright and awful morning when suddenly from a ridge ahead of them, a shot rang out!

Half asleep in their saddles, the men cursed and slapped spurs to their horses to race for shelter. And there was none.

They were caught on an open flat and the shots came from a ridge all of four hundred yards ahead, but they were accurate shots. The first burned Red Swilling's arm, the second dropped a horse, the third carried away the pommel of Lee Jaeger's saddle. The riders scattered and ran and bullets followed them in their flight.

Remounting the hard-fleshed buckskin, Kilkenny circled swiftly toward a canyon where one of the riders was headed. When he reached it he slid to the ground.

The air was still. Heat waves rippled and then gravel rattled. Then the rider came into view. "Drop the rifle!" Kilkenny held his own in his hands. "Let go your gun belt. A wrong move and I'll gut shoot you!"

The rider's unshaven face was red from the sun. His hesitation was momentary. The rifle left no room for argument. He complied with the order, careful to make no mistakes.

Taking the man's rifle, Kilkenny shattered the stock over a boulder, and jammed the action. The rider stared bitterly as his rifle was ruined.

"That rifle cost two months' wages!" he protested.

"Tough," Kilkenny said wickedly. "You'd have killed me with it, wouldn't you?"

"What d'you want with me? Dee will kill you for this! He'll never quit until he kills you!"

"Dee? That white-bellied weasel? Tell him when I'm ready for him I'll come an' get him. First I want him done brown by the sun. I don't like that pasty hide in front o' me."

The man stared back at him. "What you aim doin' with me?" he demanded.

Kilkenny smiled then. "Why, what do you think? Want a gun in your hand and an even break?"

The fellow touched a tongue to his dry lips. "That wouldn't be no break. I ain't got your speed an' you know it."

Kilkenny smiled and picked up the man's guns and cartridge belts. "All right then," he said, "you want to manhunt. I'll let you, but it won't be comfortable without a saddle."

"Huh?" The man stared, puzzled and suddenly worried.

Coolly, Kilkenny moved toward the man's horse, his eyes faintly humorous.

An hour later, several miles to the south, Spade Woolley joined Havalik and the others. He was dark-faced from cussing and was astride a horse with only a bridle, his saddle gone and his guns gone. Also his canteen was gone.

"What happened to you?" Swilling demanded.

"He headed me off an' laid for me." Woolley was sullen and bitter. "Told me I could go on huntin' but I'd be damn' sick of it.

He was right, I am sick of it, an' I hope somebody shoots me if I ever throw leather on another razor-backed hoss!"

Havalik stared at him, red-eyed and furious. "What are you? A baby?" he sneered. "Lettin' him sneak up on you? What are we s'posed to do now? Wetnurse you? No canteen, an' you'll want to drink our water, no guns, no saddle. Start for the outfit, Woolley, an' start now."

"Huh?" Woolley's face was ludicrous in its amazement. "Without a canteen? I'd die afore I got anywheres!"

"Tough, ain't it?" Havalik sneered. "That'll learn you a lesson. Get goin'!"

Red Swilling stared at Havalik. "Dee, you don't mean that! Hell, the man wouldn't have a chance!"

Havalik turned like a poised rattler. "Want to make somethin' of it? You want to go with him an' leave your canteen? Or you want to go for your gun? You got a choice o' that or shuttin' your trap an' obeyin' orders."

Red Swilling swallowed and moved his hands carefully away from his guns. Havalik was trembling with eagerness and ready to kill. Swilling was shocked and frightened. "Hell, you're the boss, Dee," he protested, "I only—" His voice trailed off.

Havalik's eyes were on Woolley. "You startin'?" he demanded. "Or do I cut you down? I got no use for a damn fool!"

Spade Woolley stared back at the man and suddenly all the years of his life came up in him to curse him. He looked into those red-rimmed eyes, and suddenly he said, "I'll go, Dee," his voice was low, "an' I hope I get through. I want to get through now just for one reason. I want to be there when Lance Kilkenny shoots your rotten heart out!"

Woolley was beyond caring what happened. He knew the nature of the man before him, could see that flat, ugly mouth, the cold chill of that still gray face, the viciousness of the man's eyes, but deep within him was the courage he had been born with. "You know what he told me to tell you? He named you for a white-bellied weasel and said when he wanted you he'd come for you. He said he wanted your pasty hide done brown before he came for you, but he was wrong, Dee, that dirty white hide o' yours won't brown. It's the hide of a dead man!" Spade leaned forward. "A dead man, d'you hear? You're dead an' you're rotten before you lie down!"

Dee Havalik's flat lips writhed suddenly and his hand was a blur of movement. The gun came up and flame stabbed, and Spade Woolley folded up and slid from the back of his horse, hitting the sand on his side, then rolling over. For an instant, his eyes flared wide. "You saved me, Dee. Saved me from dyin' o' thirst out there! But . . . but you . . . you're dead! *Dead!*" Blood frothed at his lips and only his eyes were alive, brilliantly, horribly alive. "Dead! Kilkenny will kill you! He's faster than you! He's . . . he's my kind o' man! I . . . I wish . . ."

"Mount up!" Havalik's voice was shrill. "Hit the leather! We're goin' on!"

Red Swilling stared for a moment at Havalik, his face somber with brooding realization. His eyes flicked to Baker and Grat. They were staring unseeingly at the sand. Slowly Red moved to his horse and the others followed. Nobody spoke of the dead man lying on the sand, but none of them was forgetting. And that ended the seventh day of the chase.

Kilkenny took a narrow wild horse trail that led up to North Point and then turned down the plateau. Far below him he could see the pursuers. He had heard the shot and wondered at it, but supposed a horse had broken a leg. He pushed on into the afternoon, and at night he doubled back again, locating their camp by the firelight.

From a safe distance he watched through his glass. The men's lips were not moving. They were not talking or looking at one another. Havalik sat alone, and nowhere among them was the rider he had seen this morning. Finally, one by one they crept to their blankets. Havalik was the last to go. One man remained, a guard.

For an hour Kilkenny rested. Then, leaving his horse, he crept forward, flat on his stomach. It was a slow and painstaking progress, but soon he was at the edge of camp.

The fire was dying. Straight before him was the guard, his back to Kilkenny. Beyond the fire was a low bank, some eight to ten feet high, and between it and the fire were the horses, cropping grass within plain view of the guard. East and west of the fire the men were rolled in their blankets, sleeping.

A stick fell and sparks leaped up. The guard got to his feet and gathered a few more sticks to lay on the blaze. The flames eagerly embraced the sticks with glowing arms and thin tendrils of flame and smoke crept along the length of the sticks. The guard yawned and scratched, staring around into the darkness, but Kilkenny lay among the clumps of bunch grass and was not worried. The guard had been watching the fire and would be almost blind to the outer darkness. No Indian would do that.

Finally the guard seated himself again and began to roll a smoke. Kilkenny studied the situation with care and then found what he wanted. Not far from the nearest sleeper were his saddle-bags and canteen. With infinite care, Kilkenny slid forward the stick he had brought with him and, sliding it into the canteen carrying strap, he turned it round and round, winding up the strap. Then he lifted the canteen with care and drew it back to him.

Easing back deeper into the darkness he put the canteen beside a whitish, water-worn boulder and then circled the camp. It took him more than an hour of painstaking effort and waiting, but at the end of that time he had gathered four of the seven canteens. One of those was Dee Havalik's.

When he was a good two hundred yards off, he paused. His horse was close by and he had the four canteens fastened to the saddle. Lifting his Winchester .44–40 he shot three times into the flames as fast as he could lever a rifle.

The guard dove for the outer darkness and men scrambled to get out of sight. Kilkenny reloaded his rifle and walked back to his horse and mounted up. "Come on, Havalik!" he yelled. "What's the matter with you? Can't you read signs any more?"

Behind him there was a yell of rage but he cantered off into the darkness and now he turned west and then south. At daybreak he was camped on an eminence where he could overlook his back trail. He had deliberately avoided all waterholes, having plenty of water himself, and knowing they would be splitting the water of three canteens among seven men.

Riding into a maze of canyons, he deliberately rode and rerode over his trail, confusing it purposely, then he headed out straight east and was on the outskirts of Horsehead by sundown. After two hours of rest he left the buckskin picketed on rich grass and slipped into town, making his way toward the light he saw in Doc Blaine's.

Doc was reading in his study when Kilkenny opened the door, and he glanced up sharply. "Just me, Doc." Kilkenny sat down on the settee in the shadow. "What's been happenin'?"

Blaine put his book down. He could see the fine drawn lines of Kilkenny's face, for the trials of the last few days, the sleeplessness, that heat, shortage of water and all the rest of it were plainly etched there.

"Quiet enough right now," he said, "everybody knows who you are now. Dolan told me, I don't know who told the others."

"Any trouble at the KR?"

"Some. The Forty started to push cattle on the place two days ago and ran into something they didn't like. The KR outfit had tied up with old Dan Marable and the Roots and they opened fire at long range. Knocked one rider out of his saddle, killed a horse and about forty head of cattle, laying them in a line right along the boundary. I hear Tetlow was fit to be tied. He ranted and raved for hours, but none of his boys were very anxious to try to push cattle into that straight shooting. Since then things have been hanging fire, waiting for Havalik to get back I suppose."

"He was following me."

"So I heard. What happened?"

Kilkenny shrugged. "Not much. I made them chase me, shot their camp up, stole most of their canteens an' generally raised hob just to make 'em miserable. They've had a mighty dry ride."

"We had a meeting in town and the place split right down the middle. Macy has Dolan, Early, myself and a few others on his side. Most of the town are against him, but not all."

"Has he done anything yet?"

"He hasn't tried. He wants to avoid an all-out gun battle if he can. There was an inquiry into the killing of Carpenter, but no proof. Eight witnesses testified that Carpenter deliberately ran in front of the stampeding cattle. Mrs. Carpenter said they drove them into him. That was the way it ended, and the Forty outfit walked out laughing."

Kilkenny turned his hat in his hand. "Make up your mind to

this. When Havalik comes back, he'll be killin' mad. The first man to cross his path will die. I mean it. I think he killed one of his own men out there. At least, he disappeared."

"What are you going to do?"

"What I've been doing. I'm going to move against the Forty tonight. Tomorrow night, I should say."

"Nita Riordan wants to see you. She asked me to tell you."

Kilkenny looked up quickly, then he shook his head. "Not yet. I've my own reasons." He got to his feet, then looked quickly at Doc. "How does she look? Is she all right?"

"Yes, she's looking fine. In fact, she's the most beautiful girl I ever saw."

Kilkenny nodded. "She is that. And one of the finest."

Doc Blaine had the quick perception of one long geared to the study of human reactions. It was here, too. This man was in love with Nita. As much, he decided, as she was in love with him. He felt a quick start of pain at the thought. It had been a long time since he had seen a woman who excited more than a passing interest, and Nita Riordan had—there was something about her that stayed with you after you had seen her once.

The man before him was the same sort, Blaine admitted that. Having once seen Kilkenny to know him, one was not likely to forget. He was like an edged blade, sharp, clean, and strong, yet resilient. Yes, that was it, he was resilient.

Yet he was more, too. The man had character. Curiously, he wondered about his background. This man a killer—what had started that? Badmen looking for trouble and a naturally quick hand and eye? Probably.

Kilkenny turned restlessly. He was never very comfortable inside a house. That might come, but not now. "All right," he said, as though just responding to the message from Nita, "I will go see her, but not right away. I've too much to do and," he added quietly, "I know this thing too well. Take your mind off it for an instant and you're shot full of holes. These boys are playing for keeps."

"I'd like to know what Jared Tetlow is hatching right now. You can make up your mind it's something."

"I agree."

Kilkenny picked up his hat and turned swiftly to the door. "Someone coming. I'm going."

Almost before Doc Blaine could adjust himself, Kilkenny was gone. And Doc had not even heard the door close. Or seen it open.

There was a sound of voices, then boot steps and a spur rattled. An authoritative fist pounded on the door and Blaine went to it.

Three roughly dressed men pushed their way into the room. Doc knew them instantly. They were the pursuers of Kilkenny. Havalik was in the lead. "Got a wounded man, Doc. Take care of him."

He turned swiftly and surveyed the room, then walked through into the kitchen. "You alone?"

"Yes," Doc's voice was sharp, "and stay the hell out of my kitchen, Havalik! You're here with a man for treatment, not making an inspection of the furniture!"

Havalik whirled, white hot on the instant. "Yuh talk to me that way?"

"To you or any man. You've a wounded man here and that wound's in bad shape. You stay in here and mind your own business and I'll tend to mine. I won't lift a hand until you do."

Havalik was ugly and he took a quick step forward. Calmly, Doc picked up a scalpel. "This is my business, Havalik. I could cut you open as quick as you could shoot me at this range. And I'd cut where you'd bleed to death mighty fast."

Havalik stopped, staring at the doctor. There was conviction in Blaine's voice, and it surprised Havalik to see that he meant it. He drew back.

"Furthermore," Blaine continued, "this community values my hide. They need me here. There's not another doctor anywhere within two hundred miles. If anything happens to me they'd lynch you, Forty or no Forty. And before this is over, you may need me yourself."

"What's that mean?" Havalik demanded angrily.

"It means—" Doc was working swiftly and surely. It was a nasty wound. "It means," he repeated, "that you're carrying a gun and hunting trouble. It's a combination that gets every man in the end. It will get you. I doubt if you live out the month."

Dee Havalik turned away with a snarl. The driving urge to kill was riding him, but deep inside the doctor's words rang a bell. Was it because he perceived the truth? Or because he had been accustomed since childhood to take a doctor's word for things? It made him surly, and he walked out and slammed the door, starting up the street toward the Pinenut.

Dolan stood on the steps of his place and watched him go, then he stepped off into the darkness and went down the path to the rear of his establishment. He walked swiftly to the edge of the trees, then stopped and said carefully, yet aloud, "I could furnish a good horse if a man needed a rest for his own mount, a good horse with bottom and speed."

"I could use a horse like that." Kilkenny stepped to the very edge of the woods. "Busy place around here, Dolan."

"Yeah," Dolan said dryly, "too busy. One of that outfit that was chasin' you looked in on me. What have you been doin' to that crowd?"

"They wanted to go for a ride," Kilkenny smiled, "so I took 'em for one."

"The man that hit my place was half dead. He must have drunk a gallon of water. He said he hadn't had a decent drink, not more than enough to wet his lips in two days."

"Dolan, how many boys can you muster? I mean boys with sand?"

"Enough. What do you want to do?"

"Stampede the Forty herd."

Dolan was silent, but his eyes glinted. That would be hitting them where it hurt, and right at home.

"When?" he asked then.

"Tomorrow night. They are bunching them for another push toward the KR. I'd like to run them right back over their own camp."

"That might be tough. They've too many hands."

"I've got a plan. It calls for roping a half dozen of their steers." Kilkenny suddenly was tired, more tired than he had believed possible. "I'd need about four good, solid men."

"You'll get them. Where?"

"That lightning-struck cottonwood in Whiskers Draw. Nine tomorrow night."

"They'll be there." Dolan stepped closer to him. "Man, you're all in. You'd better get some sleep. You'd better sleep until then." Without awaiting a reply, he turned and walked to a narrow gate in the corral, a very convenient gate for getting a horse into the trees without it being seen. "I saddled this gray when I first saw you. He's cornfed. He'll go all day and all night and was mountainbred."

"Good, and thanks."

"Don't thank me. Get some rest."

When he was gone, Dolan walked around to the steps again and lighted a cigar. Havalik was just leaving with his men. One man wore the white of a bandage. "What yuh mean?" this man was saying. "Yuh think Kilkenny was in that house before us?"

"I know he was!" That was Havalik.

"Think he was hurt?"

Havalik turned and his voice was low and fierce, yet clearly heard by Dolan in the desert air. "How could he be hurt? Who would hurt him? Did you see him? Did I? Are you crazy?"

"What about the Doc?"

"Leave him to me." There was icy promise in Havalik's voice. "Not now, but wait. All of this town that works against me or Forty. I'll take care of them once Forty's in the saddle."

"Dolan's place is right back there. Let's go back and bust it up and get Dolan."

Dolan took the cigar from his mouth and looked at the end of it.

"Later. He's got men with him. We'll get him when he's alone and nobody will care. Who cares about a crook?"

Dolan put the cigar in his teeth. "That's right," he muttered. "Who does?"

He was the vulnerable one. Early and Blaine were respected citizens. Kilkenny was elusive. Only Dolan could be hit without fear of retaliation. He could always, he reflected, go to Tetlow and make a deal.

He chuckled with wry humor. That was the one thing impossible for him. He could rustle cattle, plan a bank or stage robbery or hide a wanted man, but it was not in him to betray a friend or sell out a cause.

The dappled gray Dolan had given him was all horse. Kilkenny rode southwest out of town, dipped into a tangle of washes and then turned south until he finally camped with the battlements of Comb Ridge towering above him. He rolled into his blankets nearer dead than alive.

His tight muscles let go their hold, and clogged with weariness. He slept. The long hours of riding, the constant alertness, all left him and he sank deeper and deeper into a sleep of utter exhaustion. Over the hills men rode and horses moved and cattle lowed gently in the night air. Stars faded and a faint gray crept up the east, barred from him by the gigantic wall of the Ridge, a bulwark that lay across his path to the KR.

He stirred in his sleep, then relaxed. Some faint stimulus made him stir again and a violent need within him culminated suddenly in his eyes. They snapped open and for a time he lay still, unable to bring his thoughts into focus. It was a voice that did it for him. A girl's voice.

"You must have been very tired, Lance."

Unbelieving, he sat up. Nita sat a dozen feet away, her rifle across her knees, her lips widening in the quick, amused smile he knew so well.

"Where . . . where did you come from?"

"Should I be poetic, Lance? Should I say that I'm your past returned to haunt you? No, I'll tell the truth. I was restless last night. I could not stay in the house any longer so I gave them all the slip. I caught Glory—remember my black filly? I saddled her and rode west. Ever since I've been here I've been worried by this Ridge—I wanted to see what lay over here, so I came over just before daybreak and what do I find—you."

"And I didn't hear you."

"You wouldn't have heard if the Ridge had collapsed. If the moon ran into the world and they burst, you wouldn't have heard it. I never knew a man could sleep like that."

"It's lucky it wasn't Tetlow—or Havalik."

She was suddenly serious. "Lance, you're the same. You haven't changed."

"Are you saying that, or asking?"

"Both. You're the same as I see you. I don't know what you're thinking."

He got to his feet, running his fingers through his black hair which was all awry. He must look like hell. Needing a shave, tired, red-eyed, and hair all on end. How could a woman ever—or maybe she didn't. Maybe she had changed. He looked at her, trying to guess.

"You—you're so beautiful it hurts."

"Hurts who? Not you surely. You ran off and left me. I can hardly believe that. You're the only man who ever ran away from me, Lance—and the only one I ever wanted to stay."

He looked at her quickly. "You still mean that?"

"I said it, didn't I?"

She got to her feet, tall, lissome, her skin a beautiful olive, her eyes— "It's been a long time." Her eyes widened a little, and her lips parted, he could see the sudden hunger in her eyes, and he stepped toward her, half-frightened by the feeling that shook him. Roughly, he took her arms and pulled her to him and she reached hungrily for his lips and they melted together and deep within him something seemed to well up and the cold dams across his feelings were gone.

He pushed her away, her breath coming quickly, his own ragged with emotion. "It's no good," he said hoarsely, "no good at all. You've too much to waste on me. I'm a drifter, Nita, a saddle-bum, a man with a gun and a few days, weeks, or months to live. It might come tomorrow."

"It might," she agreed, "but don't you think I've thought of that? Don't you think I know?" Her voice rose. "Lance, look at the time we've lost. Yesterday, and all the days before that, the long days after you left the border country, and the days after we were together in Cedar—you know and I know we've wasted that time. I know it may not be long, and yet it may be forever. Who knows how long it is for anyone? All of us, all over the world, all of us walk along a thin edge between life and death and it takes so little for us to fall.

"It isn't tomorrow I want unless it comes. It's today, Lance! We women, we don't have so much imagination about some things. We're realistic. You think about what it may mean to me tomorrow, if I lose you. I think about what it means today, if I don't have you.

"It doesn't matter! None of it does. I know how you live, I know what drives you, and I know that maybe the Tetlows, maybe Dee Havalik, maybe someone else will kill you. Or you may kill them and have long years ahead. After all, I've known some of your like who died in bed, and you may. You think about it too much."

"I live with it," he said somberly. "What kind of life is it for a woman when her man never leaves the house walking but she'll fear his body may be carried back? If there's enough of him to carry? Sure, I've stayed away from you and I've hated it, but only because I wanted to spare you pain."

"By causing me pain? It won't work, Kilkenny. Yes, I often call you that. Everyone does. The mysterious Kilkenny, the unknown Kilkenny. Sometimes I wonder if I ever knew you myself, and if you weren't just a dream I had, and then I try to go to sleep again and I remember how your arms felt, and your kisses, I remember how you stood in the center of that room and spoke to me first. Remember what you said, Lance? You don't remember—trust a man to forget, but I remember. I remember every word you've said to me, at any time. Even the foolish little things you've said."

He looked at her and tried to find words and there were none. He watched her lips, the rise of her high breasts as she spoke, the wetness of her lips. He turned sharply away, stabbed by sudden pain. Maybe he was a fool. "I'd better get saddled," he said, "we can't stay here."

She smiled at him, laughing a little. "Tough, aren't you? Big and tough! But I know you. Under all that you're sentimental as a kid. And you love me. I've known that from the start, and that's what irritates me about you. Walking away from me!"

Nita dropped to her knees and began to roll his bed. "Get your horse. I'll fix this bedroll."

When he had the gray saddled he strapped the bedroll behind the saddle and helped her with her black mare. They both mounted and he grinned at her. "All right, you tyrant! Wake a man up looking so gorgeous it hurts! Now take me to breakfast!"

"You think I won't? And if Maria doesn't have it ready, I'll fix it for you." She led off, starting for the switchback trail over the Comb. "You know, I'm almost as glad for Cain as I am for myself. Without you he's like a big dog with no master. He needs you, Lance."

"How is he?"

"Fine, and as big and ugly as ever. You should never have broken his nose, Lance. It was probably his one good feature."

"If I hadn't, he'd have killed me. That big lug can fight!"

"I've seen him."

"Does he ever mention Abel?"

"Rarely. What was he like, Lance? I never knew him well."

"Vicious. A killer. Completely and entirely criminal, and very dominating. Cain was never bad, it was just that he followed Abel's lead. That was a good job I did, killing him. A good job for Cain if for no one else."

"He thinks so, too. And he says you were the only person who ever treated him decently, and the only one who could ever handle him."

They rode in silence for a distance and then Nita looked around at him, pausing to breathe her mare. "What's going to happen, Lance?"

"We're going to hit Forty. Tonight. And hit 'em hard."

"And then?"

"Every man for himself. Tetlow will turn loose his dogs then and it'll be kill or be killed all along the line."

"That Dee Havalik—I've seen him, Lance. He's mean, cruel."

Kilkenny shrugged. They topped the ridge and the sun burst bright in their faces. Far below them lay the ranch house and along the distant line of the two ranches was a line of sprawled dark figures, dead cattle.

Beyond them was a dark mass of gathering weight. Suddenly, he was worried. "Let's get down there! They may start something before we can!"

Suddenly the dark herd began to move and behind them, far behind them came a wave of riders firing into the air, startling the cattle. They gathered themselves and lunged, plunging across the line at breakneck speed.

Kilkenny drew up, appalled. "My God! I hope the boys aren't down there! If they are, they're dead!"

SIX

Nita caught his arm. Her face was pale. "Oh, Lance! Jaime! And Cain! The rest of them! What could have happened to them?"

"I wish I knew," he said soberly, "but we can't find out now. If Tetlow's gone this far it means he's ready to go all the way. I've got to get you out of here, Nita. Some place where it's safe."

"In town?"

"No." His mind was leaping ahead. It would not be safe in town now, not even with Early and Blaine. Tetlow had started to move and if he had wiped out the KR hands there would be no end to his killing. "No." He repeated the word. "There's another place, but we've got to move fast. Turn around and we'll go back down the trail."

"But maybe they are down there, Lance. They might be lying injured!"

He had been thinking of that very thing and the thought tortured him. He was torn between the desire to go down there and find out for himself and the need to get Nita to some safe place. She read his thoughts.

"Don't think of me. I'd be safe down where your camp was. You go ahead."

Still he hesitated, worried. "No, I couldn't go down this way now. They'd see me long before I reached bottom. We've got to circle around, and you can be sure they'll have men in Horsehead, watching for me.

"Tell you what," the thought came to him suddenly, "you take

72

that canyon"—he pointed it out from the height of the Ridge—
"and follow it up to the second branch. There will be a Y there,
but take the left-hand canyon. You'll find a switchback trail at the
end and when you come out—" Swiftly he detailed the directions
of how to get to the small blue lake he had found. "Wait there for
me. I've got a place in the mountains east of there."

"All right." It was like her not to question his judgment. "Don't
worry about me, and be careful."

They parted with a quick clasp of the hand and he turned
north, riding up Comb Wash. When he reached Whiskers Draw
he swung into it and followed along, carrying his Winchester in
his hands and riding with eyes and ears alert. He had no plan, nor
could he make one until he could view the situation that awaited
him.

There was every chance that the KR hands had been caught in
the rush of cattle or shot down by the Forty riders. There was a
slim chance they had escaped, but one scarcely worth mentioning
for they were fighting men, not running men. Their only hope in
that way, Kilkenny understood, was that Jaime Brigo was uncommonly cunning. He might have done something—on the other
hand the men might be lying helpless and injured. He had to
know and there was no time to be lost.

He had covered the miles at a space-eating gait but the gray
seemed in no whit disturbed by it. In fact, when he slowed down
the gray tugged irritably at the bit, wanting to run. At the
cottonwoods he paused. Here, tonight, he was to have met the
crowd for their attack on the Forty. Too late now—or was it?

Considering that, he shook his head to clear his mind and
returned to the thoughts of the present. This was going to be
touch and go. Without doubt the country was crawling with Forty
riders and they would be hunting Nita as well as himself. With
men on the KR, at the camp of the Forty and in Horsehead, he
would be in a bottleneck that offered but one escape, retreat the
way he had come. Dismounting, Kilkenny crept up to the side of
the draw and surveyed the country before him.

The herd had scattered, spreading over the KR range, and they
were feeding on the rich grass of the new range. Among them a
few riders rode, but they seemed to be congregating at a particular point. That point was near the KR ranch house. A few minutes

later the wagons from the Forty headquarters came into sight, headed for the KR. Obviously Tetlow was taking up headquarters at the latter house.

Returning to his horse, Kilkenny advanced with extreme caution, pausing every few yards to listen. He heard no sound, but presently Whiskers Draw gave into Cottonwood Wash, which had been the edge of the KR range, and it was along this wash that the KR hands had been holding their ground.

No sound disturbed the clear air of the afternoon. There was a faint smell of dust in the air remaining from the stampede, and the smell of sun-warmed grass. Keeping away from any stones that might make a sound under his horse's hoofs, he rode forward. When he was over a mile from the opening of Whiskers Draw he drew up. Here the wash was partly overgrown with low cottonwoods and willows, and there were some larger boulders scattered about. Dismounting again, Kilkenny spoke reassuringly to the gray, then walked ahead on cat feet, his rifle at the ready.

The first sound he heard was faint, a rustling. He paused, the rifle coming up. Then he heard a low moan, and he wheeled. The bank on the east side had been broken by the rush of cattle and had caved into the wash. Moving toward it, he saw a bloody hand projecting from under the earth.

Dropping a hand to a boulder top, he vaulted over it and landed beside that hand, and then he could see the face of a man lying on his stomach, his head turned sidewise, also projecting from under the caved-in earth.

It was Cain, and the big man was conscious. Swiftly Kilkenny attacked the pile of earth with his hands, pulling it away from the fallen man's body. Working desperately, he stopped suddenly to hear the sound of a walking horse!

Straightening up, he stared at the bank, panic sweeping him. There was no way to get Cain quickly uncovered nor to move him. A shot would bring a dozen riders, in a matter of minutes, and—he heard the horse stop, and then the creak of a saddle. Crouching among the boulders, Kilkenny lifted a finger and saw that Cain understood.

The man showed above the edge of the bank, then dropped over. It was Phin Tetlow.

A big, wide-shouldered man, he walked with easy step and he

looked curiously around. Obviously he had seen something here that he felt warranted investigation, and he had returned alone for that purpose. He looked around, then walked to a clump of willows and peered into it, then cautiously approached a bunch of boulders.

Kilkenny crouched lower, cursing his luck. He could not shoot it out with Phin and then run for it to leave Cain helpless in this position. His horse was out of sight, but further search might show it to Phin. Kilkenny drew back, easing away from Cain, and the big man watched him go, his eyes wide and trusting as those of a big dog from whose paw one extracts a thorn.

Phin was working nearer and nearer, and now he straightened and looked toward the fallen earth. Quickly, as if having an idea, he strode toward it. He paused when he came in sight of Cain. Kilkenny could see the expression on Phin Tetlow's face, and was puzzled by it.

Phin moved closer. "The big one, huh? I figured the herd must have got somebody here. I seen you a minute or so afore they hit this bank. It would have been a miracle if you was safe."

He sat down on a boulder and calmly lit a cigarette. "Can't move, huh? Well, I reckon you're my meat then. Funny thing. I never kilt a man. Andy has. He kilt eight or nine. Andy's good, maybe better than Havalik. Even Ben kilt an outlaw down in the Big Bend, and a couple of Indians. Me, I never kilt nobody."

He chuckled. "Well, I won't have to say that tomorrow. Because I'm fixin' to kill you.

"Makes a man," he said, "feel mighty small when he ain't blooded. Even Ben, an' he don't like to fight. He thinks too much." He drew deep on the cigarette. "Pap figured you for the tough one. Now here you are, caught like a rabbit in a trap. I don't even need to waste a shot. I'm going to bash your head in with a rock."

He got to his feet and stretched, and Kilkenny, close behind him now, reached out and grabbed him by the gun belt. He gave a tremendous jerk and Phin Tetlow's heels flew up and he hit the boulder hard and turned heels over head to the ground behind it. Kilkenny swung a wicked backhand blow that smashed Tetlow's nose, stifling his yell to a squealing grunt. Then he slugged him on the chin. A full, powerful swing. Phin's head snapped back and he lay still. Swiftly Kilkenny tied his hands and feet, then went to work to free Cain.

A quick examination showed no bones broken but the man was frightfully bruised and skinned. Moreover, he seemed to have lost blood from a scratch or cut in his side. Stopping, Kilkenny lifted the big man on his shoulders and started for the gray. The load was almost too much for the gray, for between them they made a weight of over four hundred pounds, but there was no help for it.

Returning the way he had come, the gray stayed with it beautifully, but when they reached Whiskers Draw, Kilkenny swung down and walked ahead, leading the horse. He might have made the attempt to get Phin's horse but had been afraid somebody from the ranch would see him up on the bank, and had not dared to take a chance as Phin had been wearing a brilliantly red shirt that could not have been mistaken.

It was slow going and hot, but he made it back to the cottonwoods. Cain Brockman lolled in the saddle, his huge body swaying to the moves of the horse. His face was gray and his eyes glazed over. Worriedly, Kilkenny spoke to him and there was no answer. The big man was sitting there by sheer will and animal strength. He might be injured internally—Kilkenny crept to the top of the bank and looked around. Far away, several miles off now, he could see the lone horse standing where Phin had left it. How long before that horse would attract attention and investigation? Or how long before Phin would get free?

It was almost noon, of course, and the hands might be eating. There was no more than another hour before the pursuit would begin, for they would notice Phin's absence and if they saw his horse, it would immediately draw them to it. What Cain needed was a doctor, but it was all of five miles to Horsehead from their present position and the last two miles would be across open country.

There was no help for it but to conceal him here and hope for the best. Alone, he could run for it, but the gray could never carry that weight over a fast run nor could Kilkenny keep the dead weight of the now unconscious man in the saddle before him.

Dismounting the wounded man, he carried him back under the

cottonwoods. Here there was a place where the willows hung low, leaving a deep shade. Here, with Kilkenny's slicker for a pillow, he made the big man as comfortable as possible. With water from his canteen he bathed the man's forehead and washe1 his wounds, leaving him from time to time to take a look around for approaching riders. Then, drawing one of Cain's pistols, he left it close beside the big man, and with him Kilkenny left his canteen.

Then swiftly he wiped out with a willow branch the cracks in the sand, and scattered free handfuls of sand over that, then mounted up and rode swiftly out of the draw and across country keeping to the cover of the cedars. When he was far enough away, he rode swiftly on and followed a dim trail that led through various draws until he was almost on the outskirts of Horsehead. Here he worked his way into Cottonwood Creek and started toward town.

This was the creek that divided east from west Horsehead, the social line of demarcation in the cowtown. It was also the draw that led through the trees past Doc Blaine's.

From the creek bed, he climbed out into the trees and then worked his way up through the brush until he was within a few feet of Blaine's house.

The first person he saw was Laurie Webster. Her eyes widened and he motioned her to silence. When she came to the fence near the trees he spoke softly. Briefly he explained what he had done, where he had found Cain and how he had left him, and told the girl to explain the change in plans to Dolan, although to keep riders on call. "Better not try to get Brockman before dark," he warned, "that country's alive with riders and they'd be sure to take him away from you and kill him, if not anybody who went after him."

"All right." Laurie was quiet. Her eyes searched his. "You . . . you're all right?"

"Sure. How are things here?"

"Bad." Doc Blaine had told her of what Havalik had said and now she repeated this. "It's going to come to a fight in town. I'm staying down here with Doc and Mrs. Carpenter. My sister is coming down soon, and I think Bob and a couple of others may move to this side of the creek. We want to be together in case of trouble."

"How's Macy?"

"All right, but he's worried. The Tetlows are in town in force now, and Harry Lott is drinking."

Lott? Kilkenny had forgotten the big marshal. A hard, cruel man. Where did he stand, Kilkenny wondered. And he knew there was no answer to that. Probably Lott himself did not know.

"I'll be back." He explained about Nita Riordan and saw the quick frown on the girl's face.

Without thinking of that, he returned to his horse and mounted. Getting around town was going to take him far out of his way. Suddenly a daring plan came to mind.

Why not ride right up the creek bed through town? Except right at the bridge it was tree-shaded and there was small chance of anyone being close unless they were crossing the small bridge. The cut was deep enough to keep him out of sight. He would be in view from the bridge for all of fifty yards before he reached it, but for only about ten yards beyond, for then the creek curved slightly to the west, then made an easy swing back toward the north and then slightly west again. In fact, the trend of the creek bed was in the exact direction he wished to go to reach the lake where he had told Nita to meet him.

Kilkenny was not a man who puzzled about a course of action. The danger of the creek bed was enormous for that sixty yards or so, and to be seen there would probably mean being trapped, yet there was less danger, although extended over several hours by a roundabout route that also entailed loss of time.

Without hesitation he put the gray down the bank once more and turned north. He walked the horse in the sand, taking his time, one hand resting on his thigh within inches of his gun butt. He paused before turning the last bend into that fifty yards of open creek and listened. He heard no sound of approaching horses, nor any voices that sounded close. Taking a quick look and seeing the bridge empty, he rode out into the creek.

They would hear his horse if anyone was close to the creek, but there were horses grazing about the town, owned by the towns-people, so that might not attract attention. They would know it was not a cow they heard for the difference in the sound of their walk is great. He had to gamble, and he accepted the gamble.

The sun was very hot in the bottom and he was sheltered from the breeze. The sweat trickled down his face and down his sides under his arms. He dried his palms on his chaps and rode steadily forward, his eyes roving. To the right he could see several trees and beyond them the roof of the jail. To the left there was only the thick clump of trees that divided the creek bed from the home of Doc Blaine.

When no more than ten yards from the bridge, he heard footsteps of an approaching man, and the slight jingle of spurs. There was nothing for it now but to continue on, and he did so, his hand ready to grab for a gun butt if it became necessary.

The walking man hove into sight and, despite himself, glanced up. It was Leal Macy.

Macy's face did not change, nor did he pause in his stride until he reached the bridge. Then he stopped and leaned on the rail, looking back the way Kilkenny had come. "Rider coming. Stay under the bridge!" he said.

Kilkenny halted and heard the horses approaching, and then their hoofs on the bridge. They drew up and stopped, and the voice was that of Jared Tetlow!

"Howdy!" Tetlow's voice was cool. "Seen that Kilkenny? We're huntin' him."

"Taking a lot on yourself, aren't you?" Macy demanded. "I'm sheriff here."

"We ain't askin' no law's advice," Tetlow replied shortly. There was a harshness in his voice that grated, yet there was indifference too. "Keep out of the way an' you won't get hurt."

"Tetlow," Leal Macy replied quietly, "I am ordering you to withdraw your cattle from the range you have forcibly occupied. If you do not do that, you will be arrested and brought before the courts."

Tetlow chuckled without humor. "What courts? In this town?" He waved a hand. "I already know your judge is back an' he favors me. So do most of the folks here."

Macy ignored him. "I'm preparing charges against you," he replied, "for manslaughter. I refer to the killings of Carson and Carpenter. You will be arrested, as will all those who participated, and you will be tried in the courts of the land. Withdraw your cattle, pay the damages we will agree upon, and I will allow you to go free on my own initiative. Otherwise, you will be prosecuted."

"Don't be a fool!" Tetlow was impatient. "What do you take me for, man? An idiot? What witnesses do you have? Who will testify against me? I had no reason to dislike Carson and Carpenter. Carson made the mistake of trying for a gun while Carpenter got caught in front of a stampede. As for my cattle, why shouldn't they move on empty range? There's no one on the KR."

"There was until you drove them off."

"Prove it."

Tetlow had spoken his last word. Clapping spurs to his horse, he rode on across the bridge into the east side of town. Dust from the disturbed planking fell down Kilkenny's neck. He started to move when another voice interrupted. He recognized the hoarse voice of Harry Lott, thickened now by liquor.

"How long you puttin' up with this, Macy? You standin' by while they run the town right out from under you? I thought you was a tough sheriff."

"I'm waiting, Harry." Macy's voice was patient. "I want to avoid a pitched battle if I can. I've seen a cow outfit hit a town like this before. I know what happens. I know how the innocent suffer. You're right, and something should be done, and it's up to us, but the time is not yet. When I can muster enough support, I'll arrest Tetlow and Havalik both, and I'll hold them for trial."

Harry Lott laughed. "Yeah? Well, you won't arrest Havalik! I got him figured! He's their backbone! Git him an' they'd blow up higher'n them clouds! An' that's what I aim to do—*git Havalik!*"

Macy did not reply and Kilkenny heard the drunken marshal's footsteps as he moved off toward the east side of town.

"Be seein' you!" Kilkenny said softly, and rode on up the creek. Rounding the bend in the creek bed, he walked his horse faster and when the last buildings were behind he pushed him into a trot.

There was far to go and it was midafternoon. He would never reach the lake now before dark. There was not a chance of it. Not a chance.

*   *   *

Near a lone waterhole high on Black Mesa, south of the KR ranch house, a big man crouched alone in the darkness, cleaning his rifle. That man was Jaime Brigo.

Hunted like an animal, he had contrived to escape. To the best of his knowledge, all on the ranch had been killed except Nita Riordan and Maria. The former had gone riding in the early dawn and so had missed the attack. Where she was he did not know, but he had infinite respect for her judgment, and she had been mounted on a good horse and had been armed. Further, he was sure he had later seen Kilkenny atop the ridge overlooking the ranch. As for Maria, she was an old woman and would not be harmed. They would need her services to care for the house.

Of Cain Brockman, Ed, and the other three men, he thought only with a dumb pain. He had known these men and worked with them. Ed he had seen go down shooting, trying to stem that awful mass of cattle. One of the other men had been roped and dragged to death by Andy Tetlow. So far as he knew, he alone was left of the KR outfit. He was an educated man, but beneath the knowledge he possessed he was first, last, and always an Indian, a Yaqui. He was basically still a savage, and his home and his friends had been attacked. Now he was moving out on his own private war.

He had no horse. He had discarded his boots and made of his saddle bags a pair of crude moccasins. Now he was starting out and he was not thinking of prisoners. He was thinking of death. Huge, powerful, and cleanly muscled, he was not disturbed by what lay ahead. In the darkness he moved out, and in the darkness he struck.

Carl Hadley was a tough young Missouri rider of the old Bald Knob breeding. He had killed three men in his time, robbed a bank and rustled a good many cows. The first job he had held had been with the Forty, and he had helped them to take over range before this. He was enjoying the power of the brand he rode for. He was happy to see the herd take over the KR. He had been one of those who looked upon the murder of Carson with satisfaction.

On this night he was riding along a dim trail north of Black Mesa. Ahead of him, a stone fell, then rolled. He rode forward, gun in hand. Above him loomed a boulder, and as he rode past it he had a sensation as of something huge and black dropping upon him. He was wrenched from the saddle and hurled to the ground.

Stunned, he started to stagger to his feet and was struck and knocked rolling. He came up and grabbed for the knife he always carried, but his knife wrist was seized by a big hand that shut down hard and the bones in his wrist crunched under that power and a scream of agony rang from his lips, and then another huge hand seized his throat and there was a brief instant of blind struggling before a darkness washed over him and he went limp and helpless.

Brigo dropped the body of Carl Hadley and walked to the horse. It shied slightly, then hearing the easy voice of the big man, it thrust out a nose at him. Brigo had a way with animals. They understood him and he them. He swung into the saddle and felt the scabbard. There was a rifle here.

Jaime Brigo started toward the KR. Somewhere his hat had been lost. The wind ruffled his straight black hair, his big jaws moved ponderously over the chew of tobacco. Enemies had moved against his beloved employer, the girl he had seen grow from childhood, whose father had meant more to him than any living being. He was counterattacking with all that was in him.

He struck again, later, with that knife, killing one of them and injuring the other. The injured man told a wild and incoherent story. Cowhands of the Forty listened uneasily and avoided each other's eyes. They were superstitious men, but sometimes things happened, and . . . two men left the Forty that night. They just rode off.

Phin was found, still bound. He could give no good account of what had happened except that the man who struck him down had been Kilkenny. Jared Tetlow knew men too well not to realize what he must do if he was to keep his hands in line. The time had come to move.

The moon was high before Kilkenny reached the tiny lake. An hour before, Brigo had killed his first man. Fifteen minutes earlier, Phin Tetlow had been found and released. News had not yet come in of the attacks by Brigo.

In town the lines were being harshly drawn. Bob Early with his family had moved across the creek to Doc Blaine's older but sturdier home, a home moreover that was backed by Dolan's. Ernleven had deserted his beloved stove and come across the creek bringing with him two finely engraved pistols and a twin-barrel shotgun. He also brought a burlap sack of shotgun shells.

In his saloon, Happy Jack sat staring at the cards he was riffling. Harry Lott had stopped drinking and was staring sullenly up the street. Aside from Macy, he had been king in this town. He was so no longer. He wore both guns and he was thinking of his own express gun upstairs in his room.

The streets were empty and still. Few men loitered around the bars and as the evening drew on, these grew fewer. Somehow the news that Kilkenny had been in town filtered through and was whispered around the bars and tables. Dee Havalik rode through in the afternoon accompanied by several men, but he had taken the road west and had not stopped in the streets.

Doc Blaine went with Dolan and Shorty to pick up Cain Brockman. They found him conscious and wary, and they got safely back to town. All he could tell them was that Nita had been away from the ranch when the Forty struck, and that he thought Brigo had escaped. He remembered Kilkenny coming for him, remembered his fight with Phin, and the beginning of the ride on the horse. He had passed out and recalled little else. He had awakened in darkness under the willows and found the gun and canteen. The rest he surmised and waited.

Elsewhere in the town people talked and there was much disputing about the rights and wrongs of the fight. And very little about the impending result. Agreement was unanimous that Forty could not lose. As the night drew on, the east side of town waited, breathless. On the west side, the people in Doc Blaine's house went to sleep with their clothing on, ready to rise at a moment's notice.

Shorty was on watch in the trees alongside the bridge. Pete was watching westward from Dolan's roof.

Kilkenny approached the lake carefully, but found no campfire, no one. Carefully he searched the place from a wide circle, but

saw no hint that anyone was there. Twice he risked being shot to
call out, but there was neither a shot nor a reply.

Daylight broke under lowering skies, and in the first light,
Kilkenny made a hasty search. He was tired and stiff from sleeping
on the ground. It looked like rain and he had no slicker, but then,
on the far side of the lake he found the kicked-out remains of a
campfire. And he found where a horse had been picketed. Searching around, he found a place where a struggle had taken place,
and then where Nita had walked away with three men. One of
those men had very small feet.

Backtracking, he found their tracks. Four riders had come
here, and three had dismounted and approached Nita's camp
while one remained with the horses.

Kilkenny paused and lighted a cigarette, carefully shielding the
glow of the match. The logical place for them to have awaited him
was right here. They might have ambushed him here when he
came to meet Nita. However, Havalik was no fool, and having
lived as a hunted man himself, he would guess that any camp
Kilkenny approached would be approached too warily. Moreover,
they had several times lost his trail before this and knew he was a
skilled frontiersman, adept at woodcraft and with all the tricks of
the trail.

So they had taken Nita and gone. To return to Tetlow? That
was their best bet, but would that be the bet Havalik would
make? He would be thinking more of Kilkenny and killing him
than of anything else. And he had no doubt those small boot-
tracks belonged to the gunman.

Mounting the gray, Kilkenny turned to trailing the party. The
trail led east into the worst of the mountains, toward his own
cabin and the Valley of the Whispering Wind!

Dolan had not been mistaken about the gray, for the horse had
a willingness for the trail equaled only by Kilkenny's own buckskin. The tracks led plainly off toward the east and after crossing
the plateau, dipped into a narrow gap between gigantic cliffs.
Here the sand was hard-packed and the hoof scars were plain as
print. Kilkenny gave some time to studying each hoof print,
knowing that upon his memory of their characteristics might
depend success or failure.

Kilkenny looked at the sky. He had left his slicker under Cain's head and had no protection against the rain. He rode on, and the trail became increasingly bad. He was not worried about Nita, for she had been born to the saddle, nor much worried about these men as long as Havalik was along, for the gunman was not eager after women. He was a man who lived to kill, and Kilkenny doubted that he even thought of Nita as anything but a pawn in the game. That might not be true of the others, but in the West few men would risk bothering a woman. It was the one thing the frontier would not accept.

A few spattering drops of rain fell, and Kilkenny dug into his bedroll and got out his ground sheet and wrapped it about him as best he could. It was cumbersome and did not help around his neck, for it kept slipping down. It did, however, keep off the worst of the rain, and it was now raining hard.

He hurried the gray, lifting the horse to a canter. If the rain continued the tracks would be washed out.

And within a half dozen miles, they were.

But not before they had told their story to Kilkenny. Havalik was hunting a place where there was shelter from the wind and rain. It showed in every deviation of the trail. He was hunting such a place, and he would not go much further. The rain eased a little, and lowering black clouds crowded down around the mountains, drifting in gray tendrils through the passes and between the cliff tops. The wind stirred and on the breath of the wind came a faint smell of woodsmoke!

It was late evening now, for the trail had been long. Kilkenny stripped off his ground sheet and rolled it, returning it to the place behind the saddle, and then he slipped into a worn buckskin jacket, but one that left his gun butts free. His mind was utterly cold, his eyes like those of a searching hawk. He walked his horse, keeping to the sand or soft earth, careful to strike no stone.

Again he paused. The smell of woodsmoke was stronger now. A gleam caught his eyes, and looking through the junipers he saw the fire. It was built in a cut back under a bulging cliff and several men stood about the fire. Their horses were picketed just beyond, and Nita Riordan stood alone on the outside of the fire.

Kilkenny hesitated for the wink of an eye, and then he slapped the spurs to the startled gray and palmed his Colt. The first shot rang out and he charged into the camp, yelling and shooting. A man spun and dropped, others dove for shelter, and Nita, her eyes suddenly alive, sprang quickly left. His gun exploding, Kilkenny hit the camp at a dead run, bending swiftly to sweep his arm around Nita's waist. Instantly, her foot sought the stirrup and then the gray was past the camp and running while the frightened horses lunged and plunged. One jerked free a picket pin and stampeded out of camp.

Behind them a savage yell rang out, then a shot, but the shot was wild. Kilkenny did not halt the gray and Nita crawled quickly behind him despite his demand that she get in front. The gray loved to run and despite the added burden, he ran now, plunging through the wet junipers that slashed at their faces and drenched them with water. Looping the reins about the pommel, Kilkenny fed cartridges into the now empty Colt.

Then he slowed the racing horse and turned swiftly right. He descended into a canyon, and rode south at a trot, then coming to a branch, he turned north again. They had been riding for not more than ten minutes when Kilkenny drew up sharply. Far off, distant in the mountains, came a muffled roar!

His face went white and he felt his breath go out of him. Swiftly he glanced right and left. On either side were the broken but unscalable walls of the canyon, and behind him for more than a mile were the same canyon walls!

He did not hesitate, but spurred the frightened horse forward. The roar grew and behind him he felt Nita's clasp tighten with fear. Neither needed to speak, they both knew it was a huge wall of water roaring down the canyon toward them at express train speed! A wall of water running off the rocks of the mountains into the canyon. And behind them, there was no escape. Before them was the water.

Nevertheless, flight was useless. Their only hope lay ahead. Rounding a bend in the canyon, Kilkenny's heart sank, for nowhere in sight was there anything that looked like escape.

Nita's arms tightened. "Lance! On the right there! Isn't that a ledge?"

It was. Swinging the gray, Kilkenny cut across to it. The path was unbelievably narrow. Dropping to the ground beside the girl who had instantly realized the necessity, Kilkenny took the bridle. "Go ahead," he said, "and hurry!"

Up she went and Kilkenny followed. It clung to the face of the cliff like an eyebrow of crumbling rock. Several times rocks fell away from under the feet of the horse and fell into the canyon, and now they were only six feet off the bottom. Yet the path switched back and led to a higher ledge, at least fifteen feet above the canyon floor. Nita turned and went up and Kilkenny got the gray to the switchback. It was close, but the horse made it, ears pricked at the trail, nostrils wide with fear at the now thunderous roar behind them. They climbed to the ledge, and Nita was already crawling into what was almost a crack that ran back in the direction from which they had come, but a crack floored with talus and wide enough for the horse. It might be a trap, but it did lead up.

Nita scrambled into the crack and mounted swiftly as an Indian, and Kilkenny followed. Nothing loath, and frightened by the roar behind it, the gray scrambled after them, fighting for hoof surface, slipping and scrambling. They gained another ten feet and then came out on a ledge that was forty feet above the canyon floor, and here they seemed to be stopped. Hastily Nita went searching about among the rocks for some means of escape, and then the roar mounted until the very mountains seemed crumbling and crashing about them. Turning, Kilkenny glanced back.

A huge, rolling wall of water, bearing great logs on its crest and tumbling them like chips, was sweeping down from the higher mountains. It was high, higher than their present ledge, and he saw at a glance they would be engulfed. Swinging his eyes to Nita, he saw her mouth wide. She must have been screaming but he heard no sound, but she was beckoning. Dragging the horse, he raced to her. She was pointing into a black opening whose floor slanted upward into the rock itself!

She instantly scrambled into it and then the wave hit. Kilkenny felt the tug on the reins as the water caught the gray. Off on one side, the full force of the blow broken by the rocks about them, Kilkenny managed to keep his hold on the bridle even as the water washed over him.

Water roared about him and he fought his way forward. Nita

had disappeared somewhere in the darkness ahead but he managed to keep a hold on the bridle. His feet were on the sand and the horse was struggling to follow.

"Lance!"

The cry was a faint sound from the darkness, lost in the thunderous roar that filled the cavern. His thrust-out hand, feeling into the darkness before him, suddenly struck wet cloth and excited fingers grasped his arm. Cowering together in the darkness, they listened to the sound of the water, the gray horse trembling beside them.

Then slowly the sound began to die and the water receded suddenly as it had come. Clinging together, soaked to the skin, they waited in the cave's darkness.

They were free. They were safe. The water was gone.

SEVEN

"**L**ance?" Nita stirred in the wet darkness. "Do you think they were killed?"

"No telling." He got up and, holding her hand, led the way down the slanting floor into the gray light of outer day. Wet and bedraggled, they looked down the canyon, unchanged except that now the sand was hard-packed and the walls were wet and dripping. Painstakingly they made their way to the canyon's bottom.

They walked on, anxious to keep moving. Slowly warmth returned to their flesh and watching ahead, Kilkenny could see they were bearing directly into the heart of the Blues.

"Where are we going, Lance?"

"Home. We're going home."

Mounting an alluvial fan, they found their way through a shattered opening in the canyon's upper wall and came out on the plateau.

Before them was the towering rampart of the Blue Mountains. Three mighty peaks loomed against the sky, and forward of their position, three more peaks. The sky was heavily overcast, the peaks shrouded in black masses of cumulus. About them the desert was gray, tufted with midnight blue clumps of shrubbery. The scene was shocking in its majesty, breathtaking in its power. The great shoulders of the mountains vanished into the clouds, the gray earth was streaked with the white trails of runoff water.

Turning, they looked over a vast panorama of foothills and valley. Despite the clouds the rainwashed air was piercingly clear, and miles to the south a few faint trails of smoke marked the town of Horsehead. Nearer the terrain was slashed with ragged canyons, ripped deep into the rocky terrain and tufted here and there with juniper.

"We're going up and through those mountains." Kilkenny indicated the vast jumble of peaks, black under the clouds.

"Now? In this storm?"

"Now," he said grimly, "right now!"

They mounted the gray, who switched his tail at the added burden. There was no trail, for they followed along a mountainside with the vast sweep of forty miles lying below and beyond them. In the distance gray rain drew a veil across the valley. Twice they passed the paths of small slides, and once worked their way through a great gully ripped from the mountain by a rush of water.

There was nothing to be gained by worrying what might happen in Horsehead. The men were seasoned in frontier warfare and he had first to get Nita to a safe place, and the only one that might be secure was the Valley of the Whispering Wind.

Despite the lateness of the hour the sky retained a strange afterglow as of distant fire, but now that had gone and they were left in utter darkness broken only by far-off lightning and the mutter of thunder among the canyons. They could go no further in the unknown darkness.

"We'll make camp," he told her. "There's some cliff dwellings near here."

He had seen the dwellings from afar, days ago. A white gash of the cliff marked the canyon.

A flare of distant lightning showed them a steep path and they stumbled up and into one of the dwellings. Obviously, the place had been used for shelter at some distant date for a few dry sticks lay near the remnants of a fire. Drawing them together, Kilkenny soon had a fire going. Roaming through the other rooms, Kilkenny found a pack rat's nest, a mine of fuel. Nita started to make coffee.

"Ruined?" He looked at the soggy mass.

"We can use it."

He dropped to a seat near the fire. Cold and wet they might be, but her very presence changed everything for him. She caught his glance and smiled. "I never imagined I'd start house-keeping in a ruin! And both of us soaked to the skin!"

Twice he went into the darkness and listened, every sense alert to the sounds of night. And he heard nothing but the wind, the rumble of distant thunder, and the occasional stirring of some small animal. He found grass and rubbed down the gray horse.

Nita was waiting with coffee when he returned, and they sat beside the fire and sipped the coffee in silence, listening to the faint hiss of the fire as the flame drained the strength from the dry wood.

Long after she was asleep on the blankets, he sat feeding the flames. Once he thought he heard horses, but after a long time of listening believed he was mistaken. Sometime after that he slept, awakening suddenly in the first light of coming day. He awakened Nita, threw sticks on the fire and went outside. When he looked into the overhang where he had left the gray, two more horses stood beside it!

Both were saddled, and one was Nita's mare, Glory. Searching for their tracks, he realized the horses had not been ridden but had found their own way here, evidently following some scent left by his own horse.

After a quick cup of scalding black coffee, Kilkenny stripped the extra horse of saddlebags, rifle, and canteen and took them to his own horse. He had just hung the canteen to the pommel when Nita spoke. "On your left. You're covered."

Kilkenny turned carefully and found himself facing Jess Baker. The cut on the big man's face was an ugly red scar. He held a .44 Colt and he was grinning.

"Never figured on no such luck. I was a-trailin' them horses. Havalik figured we might need 'em."

"Where is he?"

"Maybe eight mile back." The big man was vastly pleased. "Means I get to kill you and keep your woman."

Kilkenny turned and walked away from Nita. He knew Baker would do just what he said.

"Stand still!" Baker yelled.

Kilkenny halted abruptly. "Why, sure, Jess. Look, can't we talk this over? I mean—" He drew and fired.

That draw was incredibly, unbelievably fast. Baker had not

dreamed any man would attempt a draw when covered at thirty paces. One instant Kilkenny's voice had been pleading, a salve to the big man's wounded pride, and the next that hand blurred and flame spouted. Something struck Baker hard in the stomach and he took a step back, his eyes blinking. The gun slid from his fingers and he went to his knees, then simply rolled over and curled up dead.

All day they pushed on, higher and higher into the stormswept peaks. He had taken the slicker from the spare horse, probably belonging to the man killed when he rushed their camp.

Rain fell intermittently, washing out any trail. They topped the pass among heavy clouds and Kilkenny had to bend low from the saddle to study the earth. The way dipped down and they entered a forest rich with pine smell and the sound of rushing water. At last Twin Peaks loomed on their right and Kilkenny turned, weaving a pattern among the trees, then skirted a great rock slab and drew rein on a ledge.

Nita rode up beside him and sat for the first time overlooking the Valley of the Whispering Wind.

Walled upon two sides and almost upon the third, the valley lay between, a rolling expanse of lush green grass dotted with clumps of trees and bounded by the ridges covered with green forest. Even under the lowering clouds the valley was indescribably lovely.

"It's home," he said, his heart suddenly full. "I call it the Valley of the Whispering Wind."

"How did you come to name it?"

"Wait . . . you'll see."

A mile further into the valley he drew up and waited. Nita paused beside him.

A minute passed, and then another, and slowly she became conscious of a nameless stirring, a faint rustling through the grass and leaves. It was a sound not unlike the rushing of a fast train, sometimes heard in big timber, but something fainter, as though from wind singing in the strings of a far-off violin. A whispering wind, a singing wind.

"Hear it?" he asked gently. "When you hear that sound it means you're home."

On the day of Kilkenny's arrival in the valley, Dee Havalik returned to Horsehead.

He was in a savage mood. Kilkenny's sudden charge from darkness had caught him flat-footed. Despite their pursuit they had found nothing, and only precipitate flight saved them from death under the torrent of water. Returning to confess failure did not sit well with the gunman, nor did he like to think of Kilkenny outsmarting him. Yet rain had washed out all tracks, and the canyons were a maze.

The street of Horsehead was deserted. Nobody was in the Westwater dining room, and the stove was cold. Havalik walked out on the street with his two remaining men. No horses lined the hitch rails. The Emporium was closed and the shutters were up. Crossing to the Pinenut, Havalik shoved through the swinging doors. A bartender read a week-old newspaper and the saloon was empty.

"Where's everybody?"

"Hidin' out. A few holed up across the creek."

"Who's over there?"

The bartender shrugged. "Maybe Macy can tell you. He's in his office."

The KR, he found, had been taken. Several KR hands had been killed, but it was believed that Kilkenny had somehow saved Cain Brockman.

The news gave Havalik no pleasure. Already there was an uncertainty among the Forty riders. The strange night attacks were having their effect, and a few of them were wondering if Jared Tetlow had not overreached himself. Yet Tetlow believed the situation in hand.

Within an hour after Havalik's arrival in Horsehead, Jared rode into town sided by his two sons, Ben being with the big herd on the trail. They went at once to the Diamond Palace where they joined Havalik. A few minutes later four of the Forty riders appeared on the edge of town and rode along back streets and into the patch of woods that concealed a narrow bridge. Two more drifted into the Pinenut Saloon. Within an hour there were twenty-five men disposed about the town, filtering in so gradually that all remained unaware of any concerted movement.

All but Harry Lott. Big, unkempt, and surly, he prowled continually, and he saw things. Lott had nothing against Tetlow, but Horsehead was, he fancied, his town. His authority was being scorned.

Kill Havalik, he reasoned, and the backbone of Tetlow's power would be broken. He was seated at a table in the Pinenut Saloon when he reached this decision. He shoved the bottle away from him and began to think.

The scattered groups of Forty riders broke up and vanished and the town lay still. Harry Lott went up to his bed and turned in, resting before what was sure to come.

Dawn broke bright and lovely, but a few clouds hung over the mountains. The first riders in the street were Jared and Andy Tetlow and they rode straight down the street and across the bridge, drawing up before Blaine's.

Blaine, accompanied by Leal Macy, appeared on the porch.

"I want to see that Riordan girl," Tetlow said abruptly. "I want to make her an offer."

"She's not here, and I'm sure she will consider no suggestion of selling."

"I'll have her word for that!"

Cain Brockman limped into the doorway. He was wearing two guns. "She won't be forced into no sale, Tetlow!"

The older man's lips tightened with impatience. "No occasion for trouble. I'll buy her place."

"Like you did Carson's and Carpenter's?" Macy asked.

"What happened to them was their own fault."

"You're like a lot of others, Tetlow. You believe anything that is good for you is good for the country. You're guided entirely by selfish motives."

Macy stepped to the edge of the porch. "Now let me tell you something. If you haven't moved your cattle off the KR range within twenty-four hours, and if you haven't made restitution to

Mrs. Carpenter for damage to her property, I intend to telegraph the Territorial Governor as well as the United States Marshal."

Andy Tetlow pushed his horse forward. "Dad, we're wastin' time. Let's burn the place around their ears."

Jared Tetlow swung his horse and the two men rode back up the street and across the bridge. Phin sat his horse near the bridge, and as they passed he rode into the trees and started back.

Four riders waited in the trees back of the livery stable, and with these around him, Phin circled to the back door of Savory's. Dismounting, they trooped in through the back door and took stations near the front windows. Savory's was west of and cater-corner across the street from Dolan's and Doc Blaine's.

Six Tetlow riders moved down the main street toward the bridge, and took stations in the trees nearby. Dolan and Blaine were now covered from every approach.

Harry Lott came down the stairs of the Westwater Hotel and stopped in the lobby. He had seen Dee Havalik standing on the boardwalk in front of the Diamond Palace. Lott eased his guns in their holsters and stepped out, closing the door behind him. He was cold sober and ready to make his play. He saw himself as no hero. He was the town marshal and trouble was breaking in his bailiwick and he was going to stop it.

He walked into the street and faced about. He was a hundred yards from Havalik when he started toward him, and he had covered thirty yards before Andy Tetlow saw him. At some word from Andy, Havalik turned. His face seemed to grow tighter and grayer. "Lott," he said, "and he wants me."

Facing Lott he walked ten paces toward him. "Lookin' for something, Harry?"

"Call in your boys, Dee! There'll be no fighting today. I'm the law!"

"You were the law." Havalik shifted his position to put a big plate glass window behind him. The morning sun shone into that window. "Now you're a dead man."

As he spoke he stepped off the walk, still keeping the window behind him. As he stepped down, he drew.

Harry Lott was fast and game, but he knew with immediate

awareness that he was going to die. As his hands grasped the gun butts, the guns of Dee Havalik were coming into line.

Lott squinted against the glare. He heard the concussion of Havalik's guns and something struck him a blow in the midsection. There was no pain. His draw completed, his gun lifted and blasted sound. The window behind Havalik crashed, but the gunman took a step nearer and fired again. His third shot crossed Lott's second. Lott felt himself struck again and his eyes blurred.

Desperately, he knew he had missed. Havalik's figure seemed to waver before him, and Lott braced himself, trying to steady his aim.

Phin Tetlow leaped his horse from behind the barber shop, gun up, ready to chop down with a shot. Lott faced squarely around and shot Phin twice in the stomach, then swung back and took his last shot at Havalik and missed again.

Still standing, he used the border shift to exchange guns and peered through the blurring haze toward Havalik. "You killed the wrong man!" Havalik yelled. "You crazy?"

"Couldn't see you, saw him." The voice seemed to issue from a great distance. "One rat's as good as another."

Havalik shot again and Lott tottered forward, his gun blasting into the earth. He hit the street on his face, rolled over and tried to get to his feet, shooting as fast as he could trigger his shots. All went wild. One broke a window in the Diamond Palace, one buried in the wall within inches of Jared Tetlow, and then Harry Lott sprawled in the street, his buck teeth biting the dust of Horsehead, his guns empty.

Shaken by his near escape and the shooting of Phin, Jared Tetlow crossed the street. Phin was dead.

Suddenly, Tetlow felt old and lost. Four tall sons and now two of them killed. A bad luck country. Two dead and one disloyal. It was like him not to consider that Ben had his own intelligence, his own loyalties. Harry Lott, dying, had struck out. Unable to kill the man he wanted, he chose the next best.

At Blaine's the shooting held them still and listening. Yet news passes all boundaries and within a few minutes they knew.

South of town a rider rode up Butler's Wash and with a shielded field glass studied the cattle on the KR. A big steer with wide horns was not far from him, and only a few yards away was another. Kilkenny rode from his shelter and hazed the steers back into a cul de sac among the boulders. The grass was rich there and they would stay. He studied the other steers, and sometime later captured another.

At the Blaine house Shorty stuck his head into the kitchen and grinned at Laurie. "How's for some coffee?"

"You'll have to get wood. The doctor keeps it in that shed near the stable."

"Huh!" Shorty was disgusted. "Every time you open your mouth to a woman she puts you to work!"

He opened the door and a bullet slammed the door jamb within inches of his face. Shorty hit the steps on his belly, then scrambled back into the room. He got to his feet and glanced sheepishly at Laurie. "Looks like I won't get my coffee," he said.

Dolan and Macy had been drawn by the shot. "Looks like we're bottled up," Shorty told them. "Two of 'em out in the trees. Maybe more."

Dolan came into the kitchen. "From upstairs I could see a rider skirting Comb Ridge, high up. Might have been Kilkenny."

"Havalik went after Kilkenny and Nita with four men, and he came back with two . . . looks like he found them."

"Tetlow thought they were here so they must have gotten away," Laurie said. "I know Kilkenny has a place in the mountains. He bought supplies and a pack horse."

"I sold him the horse," Dolan said. "If anybody could make it, he could. I know the man."

Tentatively Blaine tried the door, standing well to the side. Instantly a bullet smashed the wall within inches. Shorty, crouched near an open window, fired three shots as fast as he could lever the rifle. Another shot spattered glass and he ducked flat. "Think I nicked somebody," he said. "He dropped his rifle."

For a few minutes the air was punctured with the staccato bark of guns. Then silence fell. The shooting did no damage in the strongly made house.

Doc Blaine had stationed himself in his office with Cain Brockman at the other window. Brockman was far from recovered from his injuries but his huge body was amazingly tough and he refused to be coddled.

Dolan's place was guarded by his own men, who welcomed the chance for action.

From the edge of Black Mesa, Kilkenny watched the Forty riders heading toward the KR ranch house and supper. Two riders remained on guard. The cattle moved toward the waterhole, bunching as night drew on. He listened to the distant firing, trying to imagine what was happening. The sound was reassuring. It meant that his friends were holding out. And he knew the caliber of Dolan, Brockman, and Blaine.

As dusk closed around he moved back to the gray horse and began to tighten the cinch. Suddenly he knew he was not alone. He could not have explained how he knew, for there had been no sound.

He dropped the stirrup into place, and let his eyes search the terrain. His head still lowered, he fooled with the saddle while watching the rocks.

There was no cover behind him. Yet to move from the side of the horse would leave him in the open and, considering the situation, Kilkenny liked no part of it. Only two places before him offered cover, and one of these was far more likely than the other.

Turning his horse on a three-quarter angle, he started walking on the oblique toward the rocks, keeping on the far side of the horse. Quite near, he suddenly slapped the gray, vaulted to the saddle and shucked a gun in the same instant. The startled horse leaped past the rocks, and Kilkenny, gun poised, looked into the face of Jaime Brigo.

Brigo grinned up at him. "I knew it was you, señor, but there might have been someone else near."

"You nearly got shot, compadre. Want to help me?"

"Si." The Yaqui looked curiously at the now hog-tied steers. "But I do not understand what it is you do."

"It's like this—" Kilkenny explained his plan as briefly as possible.

"Good!" Jaime said. "We will do it."

He caught Kilkenny's sleeve. "Señor? The señorita? She is safe?"

"Safe. But let's get busy. It will soon be time."

EIGHT

Swede Carlson of the Forty walked his horse slowly across the range toward the herd. The night had clouded over and the distant rumble of thunder hinted at the possibility of more rain. A hundred yards away he could see the dark outline of Slim's angular figure slouching in the saddle.

Slim rode toward him. "I got the creeps!" he said, looking around. "It's mighty dark, all of a sudden."

Swede told him about the killing of Harry Lott and of Phin. "The old man's turned mighty mean. Losin' his second boy."

"Yeah." Slim glanced over the herd. They were restless over the imminent storm. "Ben's coming up the trail with ten thousand head."

An electric current seemed to run through the cattle and as if on signal they came suddenly to their feet. One instant the night was still and then the herd was up and running. Horns clashed and somebody shouted vainly. Swede swung his head as he fought his horse around. Rushing down upon the herd was a row of dancing, leaping lights!

With one mind the herd was gone. Swede caught a glimpse of Slim trying to swing his horse, saw a charging steer hit them broadside and saw Slim and his horse go down under the charging cattle, and then he was fighting blindly, instinctively, for his own life.

Under him the pony stretched out, running desperately while Swede tried to edge him over and escape from sure death under the pounding hoofs.

99

Far behind, Kilkenny drew the gray to a halt. Brigo drew up beside him and they watched the herd go. "They asked for it," Kilkenny said, "now they've got it."

Away in the darkness, Swede Carlson finally saw an opening and lunged his horse toward it. They got out of the herd and into the brush. He stopped there, his heart pounding. A steer ran past him, fire still blazing around one horn. Old sacking and grass had been rolled together and tied between the steer's spreading horns, then set afire. Such a fire would not burn long and would blow or burn itself free before it could harm the steer. The flames had been all that was needed with the skittish herd.

Slim was dead and there was no telling how many more. It was not going to be a one-sided fight this time, Swede decided. From the town a rifle shot sounded, lost in the vast silence left behind after the rushing hoofs of the cattle. Dismally Swede turned back and began to search for the other riders. Far off, very far off, he could hear the running herd.

Ben Tetlow was riding the point of his trail herd nearing Westwater. He was tired from the long ride and was about to bed down the herd when he heard a distant thunder. He drew up, listening. A rider cantered up. "Boss," he said, "that sounds like—" He broke off, rising in his stirrups.

The sound was suddenly louder and the skyline was broken by bobbing heads and horns. Fear went through Ben like the shock of cold water. "Ride, damn it! Ride! It's a stampede!"

There was no chance to stop the rush of cattle and they rode for their lives to get to the edge of the herd. The heads of the ten thousand cattle came up, eyes rolled, and then as the shock of charging cattle hit them they wheeled in their tracks and lit out at a dead run.

Ben Tetlow stared after them. All they could hope now was that weariness from the long march would have left the herd too tired to run far.

"What started 'em?" he asked a rider who trotted up.

"Somebody tied burnin' rags between their horns."

"Kilkenny." Ben stared off to the north. "I wish Dad had never started this fuss."

The rider was Swede Carlson. "The Old Man's too high-handed, Ben."

"Phin and Andy like it that way. Otherwise he might have slowed down a little."

"You . . . you ain't heard about Phin?"

Ben turned on him. "What about him?"

Swede explained, telling what he had heard of the gun battle in the street.

Phin dead! Ben was thinking more of his father than of Phin. He himself had always been closer to Andy but Phin had been a silent, hard working man. His father had told Ben that he took after his mother, and Ben had not been sorry. The Old Man had always been proud of his big sons, and now two were dead because of the path down which he had guided them.

"Where'll it end, Swede?"

Carlson shrugged. "The Old Man's usin' his spurs too much, Ben. These folks have got their backs up. We've lost men. Two killed out on the range by nobody knows who. Killed with a knife."

"I'm going to talk to Dad."

"Won't do you no good, Ben. He's fierce mad now. And you know how Havalik is."

The day dawned hot and still. Strong as was the Blaine house, it was also a trap. Any movement near the windows drew fire. Luckily, there was plenty of food in the house, but the water was outside. During the night they had succeeded in drawing three buckets of water, but the third one had spilled, warning the watchers, who opened fire.

Nobody felt like talking. There was no relief in sight and all knew how ruthless Jared Tetlow was.

Kilkenny was hidden between two peaks atop Black Steer Knoll, overlooking the town. With him was Brigo. Vainly he searched his mind for a solution. In the town below no life stirred except around the saloon and then only when drinks were sold to riders from the Forty. Through his glasses Kilkenny could see the location of the surrounding attackers.

"They'll need water inside the house," Brigo said. "The well is in the yard."

Kilkenny could see what the Yaqui meant. The well was thirty feet from the house and surrounded by a stone coping three feet high. Once at the well a man would have shelter, but he could return only at the risk of his life.

Two riders appeared from the east and rode into town. Kilkenny swung his glasses. "Ben Tetlow, bringing news of the stampede."

Below in the town a man moved near the edge of the woods at Blaine's. "Get ready to run," Kilkenny said. "I'm going to show them they have friends outside."

He nestled the rifle stock against his cheek. Heat waves danced in the air, giving it a curiously liquid appearance. Deceptive, but not too much so. The distance was no more than five hundred yards. The stock felt cool against his cheek.

The muzzle wavered slightly and Kilkenny held what he had on the trigger and as the muzzle steadied he squeezed off his shot. The rifle leaped in his hands and the man in the trees leaped forward, hands outflung, then sprawled on his face in the clearing beyond the edge of the trees.

Quickly, before any return fire could be directed Kilkenny dusted the woods with three more shots, and swinging his rifle he sent a shot into the street that made a walking man dive for shelter. Brigo pulled back and started toward the horses, with Kilkenny following, feeding shells into his gun.

Mounted, they rode swiftly across the plateau, then up Dry Wash to the butte. A glimpse toward the town showed riders fanning out into the hills to begin the pursuit. The shots had at least drawn away the attack on the house. A few minutes later, from behind a ridge, they saw Ben Tetlow ride east with ten or eleven men.

Kilkenny drew rein. "Right now," he said, "would be a good time to get our crowd out of there. Most of the Tetlow outfit are gone."

Holding to low ground, they circled the town and rode back into Horsehead. The body of the man lay where it had fallen at the edge of the woods. "Switch saddles to fresh horses," Kilkenny said. "Buck for me."

Dolan stepped out as they swung down. "You're taking a chance, man! The town's lousy with Forty riders."

Kilkenny explained, then added, "It's time to take to the hills. We can fight from there. Stay here and sooner or later they'll get you."

Dolan took his cigar from his teeth and knocked off the ash. "Of course," he said. He turned and went inside. In a matter of a minute the corral was swarming with men.

Brigo walked to the door of Savory's and pushed it open. Two startled Forty riders leaped to their feet. They turned their heads and their guns. Brigo fired and his first shot knocked a man to the floor, coughing from a chest wound. The second took a bullet through the hand and he dropped his rifle and stepped back, hands lifted.

Brigo gestured to Savory. "Fix his hand. And stay out of this or I'll kill you!"

He walked out the door in time to see Kilkenny move into the center of the bridge. The shooting had drawn Jared Tetlow into the street and what he saw was Lance Kilkenny standing alone in the middle of the bridge. There was no mistaking the tall figure with the flat-crowned black hat.

Jared Tetlow looked down the street and felt a queer chill. Over a hundred and fifty yards separated them but there could be no mistake. The hills were covered with riders searching for this man and here he stood in the middle of town.

Defeatism was not familiar to Tetlow, yet now he felt its first premonitory wave. With all the armed men at his command he had failed to stop this man or bring him down.

"Tetlow!" Kilkenny's voice sounded like a clarion in the silent clapboarded street. "Take your cattle and leave the country! You brought this war. Now take it away or we'll break you!"

Tetlow felt the heat on his shoulders. Sweat trickled down his leather-like cheeks. He was strangely alone, and then from deep within him came a welling, over-powering fury. It was loosed in one great cry of fury at his defeat, pain at the loss of his sons, and shock at what was happening to all he had lived by. "You!" he roared. "I'll—"

Only the bridge was empty, and where Kilkenny had stood there were only dancing heat waves and a faint stirring of dust. Had he imagined it? Or had Kilkenny actually been there?

A red-headed cowhand with blunt features came into the door of the Diamond Palace. "I'll give five hundred dollars to see that man dead!" Tetlow shouted.

The redhead's eyes shifted. He remembered what he had heard about Kilkenny and drew back into the shadows of the saloon. Five hundred was a year's wages, but a dead man couldn't spend a dime.

In a close knot the defenders of the Blaine house began their retreat. Most of the Forty riders were gone from town, and those who remained had no desire to dare the guns of that tight little group. So the Blaine group rode west at an easy trot. Dolan, Blaine, and Shorty led the group. Early, Ernleven, and Macy brought up the rear. In the middle were Laurie Webster, Mrs. Carpenter, Mrs. Early, and two other women surrounded by four men from Dolan's. Kilkenny scouted ahead and Cain Brockman brought up the rear. Brigo scouted on the far flanks.

Kilkenny had chosen the little lake as their first stop with some misgiving. If Havalik returned in time he might easily move across country and intercept them.

As they neared the lake, Kilkenny waited for them to come up to him. "Drink up, water the stock and fill your canteens. We'll push on."

"Tonight?" Early glanced doubtfully at his wife's drawn face. She was not used to riding and they had come long miles since leaving Horsehead.

"Tonight." Kilkenny was positive. "It's better to be dog-tired than dead. They'll come after us and our only hope is my place."

"Do they know this lake?" Dolan asked.

Kilkenny explained about the capture of Nita at this point. He had made his plans. There was doubt that the women would stand the long ride to the valley by the route they must take. His idea was to strike due north into the unknown country, then swing west to the valley. By so doing they might avoid or lose the Forty altogether. Mounting once more, he led them north until they struck a dim, ancient trail.

It would soon be dark and he was in known country. Far off on the skyline were the Blues, but what lay between he had no idea. The night was fresh and cool and there was a faint smell of sage in the air.

When the moon came out its pale yellow light lay upon a broken land of rock like a frozen sea of gigantic waves. Knowing the restlessness of Havalik, Kilkenny rested but little, pushing on toward the north. Finally, at daybreak they made dry camp. There was a little grass and the horses ate. The women and most of the men fell asleep at once. Only Dolan seemed sleepless.

"Know where we are?" Macy asked. His own face looked tired and drawn.

"Roughly." He nodded to indicate direction. "My place is over there."

"How far?"

"As the crow flies, maybe ten miles. The way we'll have to go, twice that far."

Macy was worried. "Lance, this doesn't look right to me. We should have stayed in town."

"We couldn't." Dolan's tone brooked no argument. "It was either that or be burned out. That would have come next."

The sky was gray and the morning was cold and sharp due to the altitude. From a small peak Kilkenny studied their backtrail. Once he believed he saw far off dust, but he could not be sure.

All night his thoughts had been of Nita. Yet if she was undisturbed she would get along well. There was food, and there was water and ammunition. She was an uncommonly good shot with a rifle. She would be all right.

He could tell from the way the women got to their feet that they were still stiff and sore from the long ride. Yet there was no escape from it now. It was go on or die here. When all were mounted he led the way up the trail again. By midmorning they had crossed the flat and were headed toward a gap in the range.

There were a few cottonwoods in the bottoms, and the mountain mahogany was everywhere. Greasewood lessened and from time to time they saw a pine. Soon the number of pines increased, and twice he paused to allow the women rest. Before noon they struck an old Indian trail up the bottom of a smaller canyon. Most of the canteens were dry and the horses were suffering from thirst. A turn in the canyon left them looking up a long slope mantled with evergreens. Kilkenny headed up the slope and was overtaken by Macy.

"Mrs. Early's just fainted. We've got to stop."

"Carry her," Kilkenny said. "There's water ahead."

Macy looked doubtfully at the slope and Kilkenny indicated the Indian trail he followed. "An Indian never made a trail without purpose. And look," he pointed out a faint thread of game trail down the slope, "deer have been going the way we're headed."

Within ten minutes they dismounted beside a clear mountain stream. The water was cold and sweet. All drank and drank again, then filled their canteens.

Bob Early came up to him. "We can't go on. My wife's all in and Mrs. Carpenter is quite ill."

"All right. You're close enough and safe enough."

Picking up an ax, Kilkenny walked into the surrounding pines. Forcing his way into a tight clump of second growth, all ten or twelve feet high, he cut down several close to the ground. Then he drew the tops of the surrounding trees down and tied them together until he stood under a living hut of green. With branches from the cut-down trees he wove a quick thatch over the hut. Cain and Bob lent a hand with the thatch and soon the hut was tight and strong. Then with more boughs they made several beds for the women.

Blaine walked around the hut. "First time I ever saw that done. I'm minded to stay here myself."

"You'd better. I'll go on ahead with Brigo and Cain."

"Shorty and I'll come with you," Dolan said. "One of us can return for these people when they are feeling better."

The trail was not easy. Crossing the creek, they found themselves facing a mountainside that could not be climbed on horseback. Circling, they were fronted by an even steeper cliff. Only after several hours of searching did they find a shallow creek that could be followed higher into the timbered mountains. When it seemed they had found a way through they were stopped by a ten-foot fall.

Brigo found a way around. Part of a cave had been cut by water. The ledge at the top had proved too hard for the slow-cutting water and as the rock below was softer, the stream had cut under, forming one more arch to add to those in the area. Riding under part of the fall and getting well splashed, they went under the arch and clambered up a steep rock slope and found good going before them.

They emerged suddenly into the valley not fifty yards from the house. Nita was standing on the steps looking toward them, a rifle in her hands.

Her recognition was immediate and she turned at once and went back into the house. When she emerged they were swinging from their saddles. "I've coffee on, Lance. It will be ready in a few minutes."

He could see the relief in her eyes and he pressed her arm

gently. As the others looked around he quietly explained the situation. Brockman had sat down at once, his face showing the exhaustion of the long trip after his injuries. Only his great strength and iron resistance could have stood up under the punishment.

Shorty remained only to eat and to rest a little. Then he mounted up and started back.

The night came slowly and the dusk seemed to remain over long. Kilkenny had gone to sleep in the bedroom, exhausted after his long ordeal, almost without sleep. Dolan sat with Cain and Brigo on the steps, watching the shadows gather under the lodgepole pines. The air was cool at that altitude and hour, but none of them thought of going inside.

The situation was brutally apparent to them all. They had gained a respite, but Jared Tetlow would never stop until they were dead. Not only had he lost a second son but he had been thwarted, and it was galling to a man of his ego and firm belief in his own strength and rightness.

Horsehead lay quiet. In the lobby of the Westwater Hotel, Jared Tetlow sat in a huge leather chair, his face old and bitter. Several heavily armed men loitered on the steps outside.

The town was his. The range was his. He, Jared Tetlow, had taken them and he would hold them. Yet his cattle were scattered, two of his sons were dead, and he had lost men. Jared Tetlow knew nothing of military tactics. He did not know that the end result of all tactics is not only victory but the destruction of the enemy's power to strike back.

Yet, despite his victory, some subconscious realization of his position left him uneasy. Despite his possessions of the range and the town, Kilkenny was alive. Brigo and Cain Brockman were alive. Dolan, Blaine—all of them had gotten safely away. They would not run. He knew fighting men when he saw them and he knew they were not defeated. They would be waiting somewhere for a chance to strike again. And so these men outside guarded him.

Two of his sons remained. Andy, the tough one. The gunslinger. And Ben, the quiet one. Perhaps, the thought came unbidden to his mind, perhaps Ben was right after all? It galled him to think of Ben being right, yet looking back down the years it had always been Ben who talked prudence and peace. And he was the only cattleman of the lot. Phin had never been more than a steady worker. Bud had been a trouble hunter, Andy the fighting man. But it was Ben who had managed the herds, sold the cattle, assured their prosperity.

Jared Tetlow stared at his gnarled hands and a kind of anger welled up within him. No matter. Their cattle were here, on good grass, and no gunfighter could stop him. This would pass. He would win, somehow, and time, like the grass, would cover all scars. If the law did come in he would show them his herds, his ranch, and the quiet countryside where before there had been only these shabby holdings. This was a land for the strong, and he was strong.

He got up from his chair and strode across the room. His own cook was in Ernleven's kitchen, but the food was merely rough ranch fare. Why had the big Frenchman chosen to join Kilkenny?

The waitress had refused to come to work and the stores had not opened. He held the town in the palm of his hand but the town was an empty shell.

Happy Jack Harrow walked into the dining room, looked around, then swore. Tetlow glanced up. "Set down. There'll be grub soon."

"Yeah? But what kind of grub? I'm no chuckline rider!"

Tetlow did not resent the remark. "Seen times I'd been glad to get it."

"Any news?"

"No."

"They got away?"

"Seems like."

"Why not let 'em go, then? What'll you do if you get 'em?" Harrow had not slept well. He was doing his own worrying now. He had not sided with Early, but he liked the man, and he liked his wife. Doc Blaine was solid, too. Looking around him Harrow found no comfort in the situation. "What about the women? Do you plan to murder them?"

"Hush that talk," Tetlow replied irritably. "What has to be done will be done."

Tetlow shifted irritably in his chair. For the first time he began seriously to think about the women, and they worried him. He had never been able to cope with women. He had never been able to cope with his wife.

"You'll never keep them quiet," Harrow said, "and Mrs. Early comes of good family. If anything happens to her there will be questions asked. And if they talk there will be a United States Marshal out here."

Jared Tetlow was not worried about the marshal. Let him win this fight and there would be no witnesses to accuse him. He did not like troubling women, but Harrow's wandering comments decided him. The women must die.

He had seen a man hung for striking a woman. He had seen Western men hunt down men who molested women. He knew the rage he could incite by any move against the women. But they were in the hills. Who knew where they were now? And if they did not come back, who could say what happened to them?

Yet he did not relish the thought. How had he gotten into this corner, anyway? "If they turn Kilkenny over to me I'll bother them no longer," he said.

"Fat chance!" Harrow scoffed. "And if you had him you'd wish you'd never seen him." Harrow leaned toward the older man. "Tetlow, call off your men and gather your herd. Head west for new country. Then this will all blow over."

Tetlow turned his head sharply. "Be damned if I will! This is my country now! Here I'll stay!"

"You'll stay then." Harrow accepted the plate and cup from the cook. "They'll bury you here."

Tetlow stared at the beef and beans, feeling old and tired. Why had he come out here? What had gotten him into this mess? Would there be no end to killing? Yet now he could not stop. Irritation filled him. He stared at Harrow. The man was nobody. He had swung to his side quickly enough, and at the first intimation of change he would swing again. There was only one answer now that it had begun.

Kill them.

Kill Harrow, too. Once he would have been appalled by the thought. He only killed in battle. Now these were merely insignificant humans who interfered with him. Harrow had succeeded in making him realize what he had subconsciously known all along. There could be no safety for him as long as any of them lived. Bob Early was a strong, capable man. Leal Macy was a duly constituted officer of the law. Their words would carry weight and outside people did not realize the circumstances here.

He got up suddenly and strode to the door. "Ernie, take this note to Havalik!" He scratched words on a bit of paper. When the man was in the saddle he returned to the table.

"You're right, of course. They'd talk."

Something in his tone made Harrow look up quickly.

"You told me so yourself," Tetlow said, watching Harrow almost absently. "I can't leave them alive."

A man stood in the doorway with two guns. Harrow stared at him. If Tetlow would kill those women then his own life wasn't worth a plugged nickel. His appetite gone, he sat over his food trying to think of a way out.

"Well," he tried to keep his tone casual, "I'd better check on my bartender. I can't trust him too much."

Jared Tetlow looked up at Harrow as he got to his feet, and at something in his eyes Harrow felt a faint chill go over him.

Why had he been such a fool as to straddle the fence? You never could, not when the chips were down. He turned on his heel and walked to the door, his spine crawling. Jared Tetlow watched him to the door, then got to his feet again.

"Jack?"

Harrow turned and saw the drawn gun in Tetlow's hand. He grabbed wildly for his own gun, but Tetlow fired, the crashing report louder in the closed room. Happy Jack Harrow's knees folded and he went down, rolling over on the floor, the half-drawn gun spilling from relaxed fingers.

The man with the two guns had stepped inside. "Bury him," Tetlow said. "He was going for the U.S. Marshal."

He sat down at the table again and the acrid smell of gunpowder mingled with the smell of fresh coffee.

NINE

The killing of Jack Harrow did not pass unnoticed. Men who had remained on the sidelines saw it with misgiving. East of Horsehead two Forty hands came together on a little branch that emptied into the Westwater.

"Tetlow killed Harrow."

"Hear he figures to kill them women, too."

"The Old Man's losin' his grip. Killin' in a fight, that's one thing. Massacree, that's another."

The first cowhand wiped his mustache with the back of his hand and took a sidelong glance at his companion. "Personal, I ain't goin' to have no hand in it."

"Sort of been thinkin' thataway myself."

"I got two months comin'."

"So've I, but if we try to draw our time there'll be trouble."

The first man waved a hand at the scattered cattle. "They'll never git 'em all rounded up, an' they'll pay your wages. Cross country, it ain't so far to Santa Fe."

"What are we waitin' for?"

Two cowhands and two hundred head of cattle headed south. Before noon three other riders came upon the trail. Being skilled readers of sign, they recognized the horse tracks and read the story in the dust.

"Not a bad idea," one of them commented casually. It took no more than minutes to reach a meeting of the minds. Cattle and men made a new trail.

In Horsehead Jared Tetlow heard the story from Andy with

sullen fury. Had it been Ben who reported the stolen stock and the vanished riders he would have waved him aside and stomped out to begin a chase, but this was Andy, the tough one.

He could see only one way out. Wipe out all opposition and then go after the rustlers and cattle.

"Pick fifteen tough men," Tetlow said, "mount them on the best. Promise each one hundred dollars cash when the job is done and take them to Havalik. Tell him I'll give him forty-eight hours."

Dee Havalik received the reinforcements with satisfaction. With Andy and several others he squatted beside the fire. "Three times now Kilkenny has disappeared from a place due north and a mite east of here. That means he's got him a hideout in the Blues. He's got a good bunch of fighters with him but they've women to worry about. We can use fire to bluff 'em into surrender. But first we've got to find them.

"Andy, you take five men and head up Mule Canyon. Better keep a rider on each wall as you advance, scoutin' the country. Watch for trail sign. Grat, take five more men and ride east until you find a pass. When you do, go over and ride for the nearest bottom. Then wait for us. If we follow true courses we'll meet back in there and by then we should know something."

Havalik led his own group along the western flank of the mountains roughly opposite the trail the searched-for party had left a few days before. When he came to the rough country around Cottonwood Creek, they turned up the Blues into higher mountains. At the point where they turned they were less than three miles from the waterfall under which the party had ridden to find the back door to the Valley of the Whispering Wind.

By nightfall the three parties had come together, camping on a branch of Indian Creek. Due north of them towered the Twin Peaks, and beyond the peaks lay the valley.

Grat swung from his dusty horse and crossed to where Havalik and Andy conversed in low tones. "Struck a trail!" he told them triumphantly. "In that pass a little south of here. The rain washed out some of the tracks but two or three were that mare the Riordan woman rides."

Havalik spat with satisfaction. "Good! Good!" He nodded affirmation. "That fits. Must be the trail we lost."

"That ain't all. We found Jess Baker."

"Dead?"

"Uh-huh. Right through the center. He had his chance, too."

"Kilkenny." Havalik paced off a few steps. "I'd have give ten to one that was what happened to Jess."

"You got any ideas?" Andy asked.

"We know they came this far. From the way they appeared and disappeared it can't be much further. It could be in the mountains right around us. From now on we ride careful."

The wind whipped the fire and blew hard in the treetops. The air was cold and the sky spotted with clouds. Dee Havalik walked to a big log and sat down. What would they say in the Live Oak country when they heard he had killed Kilkenny? He had always known they would meet some day. He only hoped it would be face to face, man to man, and not in a general fight where the killing might be attributed to others.

Cain Brockman rode up to the cabin shortly before midnight. He went to the nest of rocks and trees beyond the spring where Kilkenny had bedded down after his brief rest in the house. "Lance?" he whispered.

"I'm awake."

"Spotted a couple of fires on Injun Crick, looks like. Brigo's gone down for a closer look."

"Two fires? Close together?"

"Uh-huh. Means a big bunch."

"Who's on the peaks?"

"Shorty. It took me nigh an hour to get back down."

"All right. You get some sleep."

He lay there, hands clasped under his head, studying the problem. The expected attack would come tomorrow and it would be with all the force Tetlow could muster.

There was movement near him and he caught a faint breath of Nita's perfume. He sat up and she moved down beside him. "What is it, Lance?"

"They are over the peaks. We'll have trouble tomorrow." He ran his fingers through his hair. "I'm tempted to hit them tonight with an ambush."

"Don't do that. Let them start it."

"When this is over, Nita, will you go back to your KR?"

"Not unless you send me."

"It will be cold and lonely up here in winter."

"I don't care! I'd love to see those peaks all covered with snow!" She listened to the wind. "In this valley with you? Riding, working, walking together, I'd want it more than anything, Lance."

"You'll have it, then. I'm through running. This place here in this valley will be my last stand. I made up my mind when I came here."

Nita was suddenly thoughtful. "Lance, I'm afraid."

"Of Tetlow?"

"Only a little of him. Mostly of Dee Havalik."

Kilkenny leaned back and began building a smoke. "Don't let it bother you. I don't."

"That's easy to say."

"Yes," he admitted, "and this is what I've tried to save you from without much luck. But Havalik will get more than he bargains for. He never bucked a combination like this before, and so far we've just defended ourselves."

Her mind shifted. "I think Laurie likes Doctor Blaine."

"She'd be a fool if she didn't. He's a rare sort of man."

"So are you."

"Me?" Kilkenny chuckled, then drew deep on his cigarette. The glow was bright in the darkness and Nita momentarily caught the strong lines of his face, somber and brooding. "Maybe."

The moon was rising above the wind-worried trees. They sat hand in hand, her head against his shoulder. The faint smell of tobacco smoke mingled with that of wood smoke and pines. The peaks were a hard, serrated line across the face of the moon.

Someone stirred, and with a start, Kilkenny realized it must be Taggart. It would be two o'clock in the morning and he would be going to relieve Shorty.

Kilkenny reached for his moccasins. "Better get some sleep. I'm going to scout around. Brigo isn't back."

"Don't worry. He has a sixth sense, like a wolf."

He buckled on his gun belts and picked up his Winchester. Taggart waited for him. He was a tall man, lean-jawed and haggard of face. "I'll walk along," Kilkenny said. "Brigo's been gone all night."

"That Yaqui never sleeps."

They mounted and rode away together. "Figure the fight will come today?"

"It'll start."

"I want one shot at that Tetlow."

Surprised at the tone, Kilkenny glanced at him. "You sound like you had a personal grudge."

"Knowed Tetlow since we was boys together. Before he owned one cow I had a nice ranch back in Texas. He stole my cows, burned me out, took my range."

"He's been hurt himself, now. Lost two boys, his herds scattered, his men shot up."

"He'll never quit."

They parted at the trail to the peaks. "Tell Shorty to get some sleep and to get the crowd up by five, ready for trouble."

There was a dim trail east of Twin Peaks, winding around the mountain toward the place where the fires had been seen. When he was still some distance away he swung the buckskin to a thicket and left him tied.

He heard their voices before he reached camp. Then a pistol barked, and a louder voice taunted, "Hell, Grat! You never even touched him! Bet I can notch his ears!"

Kilkenny slid through the brush, easing branches aside and moving close to the edge of the firelight. Then he peered into the clearing.

Jaime Brigo was tied to a tree and men were sprawled on the ground eating breakfast. Grat and two others were standing with drawn pistols facing the tree. The big Yaqui watched them, his contempt obvious. Blood from a scalp wound trickled down his face. Havalik sprawled on the ground nearby, looking on without expression.

The man who offered the bet lifted his gun. As he did so, Kilkenny stepped into the open, his Winchester at his hip. He held the gun on Havalik, but his command was for them all. "If you want Havalik dead, just make a wrong move!"

Caught unawares, all remained without moving and Kilkenny said quickly, "You! With the pistols! Drop them! Untie that man and make it quick or I'll splatter Havalik's skull all over your breakfast!"

Havalik sat very still. He was no fool, and he knew one wrong move would kill him. "You won't get away with this, Kilkenny. I'll have your hide."

"You'll get your chance all in good time."

He saw Brigo step away from the tree, rubbing his arms to restore circulation. Then the Yaqui picked up his rifle and buckled on his pistol belt. He turned his big head toward Grat. "This man shoot at me," he said. "I want him."

"I'd like nothin' better!" Grat challenged.

"All right." Kilkenny knew Brigo. Few could face him in any sort of hand-to-hand combat. "Walk out beyond the fire. Now all of you turn to face them. Your backs will be toward me and anyone who wants to die will have an easy chance."

Grat was a big, strongly built man. He looked from the Yaqui to Kilkenny. "You mean I can fight him?"

"Choose your weapons. Gun, knife, or bare hands."

"Knives!" Grat said, smiling with cruel satisfaction. "I always heard Injuns were good with knives but I never saw one yet who was! I go for a Bowie!"

Both men put off their gun belts and with knives held low, cutting edges up, they circled warily. Grat was a powerful, quick moving man and he had stripped off his boots for better footing. Grat moved suddenly, but Brigo caught the darting blade on his own, and deflected it. Grat lost balance and fell forward.

The Yaqui stepped back carelessly, his face hard with contempt. Angered, Grat lunged again. Like a chaparral cock with a rattler, the Yaqui began to bait him. He left openings, he appeared to slip on the grass, he circled and feinted, moving to draw Grat in.

Suddenly, Brigo lunged and the edge of his knife left a thin red line across Grat's cheek. Blood welled to the surface and began to trickle. Grat rushed and the Yaqui sidestepped away and the point of his knife flicked the biceps of Grat's left arm.

"Hah!" the Yaqui grunted as he moved away. "You wish to kill. How does it feel to be living, but upon the edge of death?"

Grat was sweating now. He was frightened, knowing that his knife skill was puny compared to that of the man he faced. The big Yaqui moved gracefully, easily, unwearied. Brigo's knife was like a snake's tongue, darting . . . darting . . .

The point flicked again at the biceps, the edge touched Grat's ear. Where the knife touched there was blood.

Grat threw caution away. His only chance was to rush, to close with the Indian before the loss of blood weakened him. He rushed, and Brigo met the rush, knocking aside the knife arm and thrusting, low and hard into Grat's belly. Eye to eye they stood, then Brigo threw him aside.

Grat landed on his knee, and instantly threw his knife, but Brigo had already moved, and throwing his own knife as Grat tried to turn away, drove it to the haft in Grat's kidney, the point driving up.

Screaming, Grat caught at the haft of the knife and tried to jerk it free. In this position, he could not exert the strength and he staggered like an insect on a pin. Brigo walked to him and, putting a hand on his shoulder, he withdrew the knife. Without looking at the dying man he wiped the blade clean in the sand. Then he belted on his guns once more and picked up his rifle.

"You are fools," he said. "As he dies, so will you all!"

Surprisingly, Macy, Taggart, and Dolan stepped from the brush. Worried by Kilkenny's plan, Taggart had started them along his trail.

Supported by their rifles, Kilkenny and Brigo disarmed the Forty riders. Kilkenny took the guns from Havalik's holsters. "I'm going to unload these," he said, "and give them back. One day we'll meet and you'll want your own guns."

Taking Havalik's hat, he spun it high in the air. Then, slip-shooting with Havalik's guns, he emptied them into the spinning hat. Then he tossed the guns into the grass at the gunman's feet.

Mumbling, the Forty riders started for their horses, minus guns, ammunition, and gunbelts. Then as they rode away the men from the valley walked into the trees toward their horses, taking with them all the guns but the two returned to Havalik.

In the pass, Havalik drew rein. "We're not goin' back. Dave, you take Joe and get to Horsehead. Get guns and come running. We're not through here."

Leal Macy stepped into the saddle and then turned. There was resolution in his jaw. "This has gone far enough! We're going into town and I'm going to arrest Tetlow. I'm going to deputize the lot of you right now!"

Dolan glanced at Kilkenny. "What do you say, Lance? This might be the time."

Kilkenny hesitated, weighing their chances. "All right. Brigo can stay here with Doc Blaine, Early, and a couple of men, just in case. The rest of us will go."

At the ranch they wasted no time. Leal Macy and Kilkenny would head the group for town, taking with them Dolan, Cain Brockman, Shorty, and Taggart. It was a good, hard-fighting crowd.

Kilkenny led off toward town, but he had not gone far when they intercepted the trail of the Havalik men. "Only two men went to town! Havalik and the rest have stayed in the hills!"

Macy's face was a study in uncertainty. "Do we stay or go?"

"We'll go on," Kilkenny said. "We'll trust to Brigo."

"My guess is that those two have gone after guns. If we get along fast we can take them along with Tetlow."

Day was breaking when the party rode into town. They tried no subterfuge, but rode right into the street. The only horse they saw wore the 4T brand. The center was at the Diamond Palace.

"Dolan, you and Brockman go down the street and pick up anybody that's loose. Taggart, you and Shorty cover the street."

Kilkenny turned toward the Palace with Macy. "You think those two beat us here?" Macy asked.

"Doubt it. I know the trails better and we pushed our horses."

Only one Forty hand was in the Palace. He was eating, but when he saw who had come in he dropped his fork. Two guns covered him and he attempted no more. In a matter of minutes he was hog-tied.

"Where's Jared Tetlow?" Macy demanded of the bartender.

"Don't know, but if I was you I'd dust out of here."

"I'm sheriff, in case you've forgotten. You make a move from behind that bar or help in any way and I'll arrest you for complicity."

Leaving their captive with the men on the steps, Macy started for the Pinenut. A shot sounded down the street and Kilkenny ducked across the street and ran into an alleyway between Bob Early's office and the harness shop. Running to the back of the Westwater Hotel, he opened the door and stepped quickly inside.

Jared Tetlow stood in the front door staring into the street. Beside him was a big man with hair the color of corn.

"You're under arrest, Tetlow! You'll stand trial for murder and theft!"

The old man stiffened, then turned slowly. His face was white and the bones stood out against the skin. "You? Arrestin' *me*?"

"I'm a sworn deputy of Leal Macy, county sheriff. Both of you unbuckle your guns."

The big young man was wide-shouldered and strong. He wanted to take a chance, but there was no chance. Carefully he let go his gun belt and, after an instant's hesitation, Tetlow did likewise.

Gathering up the guns, Kilkenny led his prisoners into the street. Macy stood in front of the stage station with a Winchester, looking across the bridge into west town.

"Brockman had trouble," Macy explained. "A man named Harper. He was dead before he hit the floor."

When Tetlow and the light-haired man who proved to be Swede Carlson were jailed, the posse turned to and made a clean sweep of the town. They rounded up but six scattered riders from the Forty. There was no sign of the two men Havalik had sent for guns.

Leal Macy worked swiftly. He sent three wires by the noon stage to be telegraphed from the nearest station informing the governor of what had happened and the steps that had been taken.

He was behind his desk and Kilkenny was loafing in the office when Ben Tetlow came in. "I understand you've arrested my father?"

"That's correct. He'll be held for trial."

"Is there any charge against me?"

"Not so far."

"Do I get to see my father?"

"No reason why not."

Ben Tetlow unbuckled his guns. He glanced at Kilkenny. "What's your part in this?"

"Deputy."

"A killer!"

"Might call me that. I never hunted trouble."

"I suppose," Ben said bitterly, "you'll kill my father now?"

"Don't build trouble where there is none," Kilkenny replied quietly. "Your father tried to ride us down. He'll get what's coming to him . . . legally."

There was a sincerity about the tall rider that convinced him. Without replying he went down the hall.

Jared Tetlow appeared to have aged, but his eyes were hard as marbles. "Son! Ride for Havalik! I want out of here!"

"You mean to have him take you out? By force?"

"Don't be a fool!" Tetlow said irritably. "How else would he get me out?"

"You're to stand trial."

"*Me?*" The old man's face was bitter. "Jared Tetlow tried like any common criminal? I never figured I'd hear a son of mine say a thing like that! You git out of here and git Havalik!"

"I'm staying out of it, Dad. I'm staying out because when this is over you'll need money and a place to come to. I'll tell Havalik you're here, but I'll have no part in breaking the law."

There was something approaching hate in the eyes of Jared Tetlow as he watched his son walk away. Then he turned angrily and walked to the bunk.

Ben picked up his guns. "Any law against moving my cows?"

"Not at all," Macy said, "but your herds will have to be cut to get out the stock belonging to other ranchers."

Ben nodded seriously. "Fair enough. I'll cut all I can with the few hands I've got. You can cut them again whenever you like."

"There's a place west of Comb Wash called Texas Flat. You could hold your cattle there with the ridge as east fence." Kilkenny gave him directions for moving the herd.

"Thanks." Ben felt uncomfortable with these men. He started to leave, then hesitated in the door. "That Carpenter affair," he said, "I had nothing to do with any of that."

"We know it." Macy looked up from his desk. "We've no trouble with you, Ben."

"That Carlson you have in there," Ben said. "I don't think he was in this."

"We'll see," Macy promised. "If he had no part in it we'll turn him loose."

*   *   *

Suddenly as it had begun the trouble was over. Business in Horsehead resumed, and the arriving and departing stages began to bring in drummers and other passengers. An official arrived from the governor's office to hear the evidence and make report to the governor himself. It was announced that a special court would be convened to sit on the case.

Jared Tetlow remained in jail. Neither Dee Havalik nor Andy Tetlow put in an appearance. The party from the valley returned to town and Nita Riordan retained Bob Early to represent her and Mrs. Carpenter. Smoke rose lazily from the chimneys of the town and the days started brightly from frosty mornings. The KR range was grazed by its own cows. The big herd had been split and was fattening on range west and south of town.

A lawyer named Jaeger arrived from El Paso to defend Jared Tetlow after it had been recommended that he be held for trial on a dozen charges including the murder of Jack Harrow. Ben Tetlow rarely came to town. Only at the end of the month did he come to see Kilkenny. He found him at the Westwater, dining with Nita.

"You said something about buying cows?"

"That's right. Will you sit down?"

Hesitantly Ben reached for the chair. "How many could you use? We need cash."

"Depends on the price. I'll buy as many as I can afford."

"I'll make the price right." Ben explained, "We'd have to drive at least a hundred and fifty miles to sell. We'd lose beef and we haven't the time."

They talked, straightening out the details of the bargain. Kilkenny contracted to buy one thousand head of the 4T cattle to be delivered on his range in the Valley of the Whispering Wind. Ben's stiffness left him slowly. He found nothing but friendliness in either of them.

When he was gone, Lance looked across the table at Nita. "Well, honey, we're back in business."

"Will you go with him on the drive?"

"Sure. I'll take Cain and Shorty along and once the cattle are in the valley they'll make no trouble." He put his hand on her arm. "I'll leave them there and come back for you."

There was a shadow of worry in her eyes. "You're still thinking about Havalik?"

"I guess so. Brigo saw tracks of a dozen riders in Dry Wash two days ago. Ben hasn't said anything but I know he's lost cattle."

"Would they rustle from him?"

"They wouldn't consider it rustling. Andy's with them, and he owns part of the cattle. They still consider themselves part of the Forty, anyway."

"Do you believe Havalik will leave once Tetlow is sentenced?"

"No." Kilkenny knew he must reply honestly. "No, I don't. Havalik will never leave until he faces me. Dee Havalik intends to kill me."

TEN

Ben Tetlow was waiting on the edge of Texas Flat when Lance Kilkenny rode the buckskin toward the herd. He looked tired, and his face was shadowed with worry.

"We cut the herd for you," he said. "It's mostly young stuff."

Kilkenny studied the cattle with care. The herd was not so tightly bunched that he could not make a fair estimate of what he was getting. Obviously, Ben had made no attempt to saddle him with a lot of culls. These were good stock.

"They look all right to me," he said. "I'll take your word for the number."

Tetlow turned to instruct his riders, and Brigo rode up to Kilkenny. "A full thousand, señor. Perhaps even more."

"Thanks. See you in a couple of days."

Ben rose in his stirrups and yelled and the riders moved in on the herd. Slowly it began to move. As always, Kilkenny felt a lift at the sight of a great herd in motion. And soon these would be his cattle, on his range. He would, for the first time, be a man of property. He was through running. Here he would make his stand.

"This a good place you've got?" Ben asked as he joined him at the point.

"Best range in the country. I'll have to cut hay for winter feeding, but I've good meadows and the range I have will carry more stock than most Western range. There are some valleys branching off that can be fed off, too."

They rode in silence for several miles. "What will happen to Dad?" Ben asked suddenly.

"I can't guess. Feeling is changing in the cattle country. They want law and order now, and they'll go a long way to have it. Lots of nesters coming into the country and they'll welcome a chance to see the issue decided in the courts."

"This change you speak of. Won't that make a difference to men like you and Havalik?"

"We're as outmoded as the buffalo. That's why I'm buying cattle. I'm going to work my stock and stay out of trouble."

Kilkenny's eyes went to the narrowing gap between Texas Flat and North Fork. Cain Brockman, as if sensing his thought, suddenly rode past them, cutting over toward Texas Flat, and Shorty rode into North Fork. Both searched the rocks and brush with drawn guns.

"Nothing stays the same," Kilkenny said. "A man has to go with the times. No man can put a rope on the past and hope to snub it down. The best thing is to learn to ride the new trails."

He glanced at Ben. "You've learned."

Ben shrugged. "Dad says I take after my mother."

"Maybe. You were the first in your generation. You'll have kids and most of them will go the way you do."

From Texas Flat the trail mounted to Long Point and led over the route taken by Kilkenny on previous occasions. By nightfall they would be at Duck Lake. From there a trail led east into the mountains and thence to the valley. Now that there was no pursuit and no necessity for keeping the valley a secret, they need no longer use the devious routes.

By high noon the drive was passing through the Notch. On the far side they paused for lunch and Cain Brockman rode up to Kilkenny and swung from the saddle. His heavy jaws were unshaven and he looked tough and rugged as always. He moved over to Kilkenny, his huge bulk moving with the ease of a big cat. He dropped on his haunches.

He jerked his head toward the west. "They've spotted us. Fresh tracks over there."

"How many?"

"Five in that bunch. Shorty saw somebody over east, too."

Kilkenny finished his plate and got to his feet. He walked over to where Ben Tetlow sat with his men. "I don't expect any of you to do anything but handle cattle. Havalik is out in the hills with a bunch of riders. You leave it to the three of us."

His eyes swept the group. These men had all been Forty riders, had worked beside those men in the hills. On the other hand, these were the best of the lot, cowhands rather than gunmen. And the drive and day to day work had enabled them to see the kind of man Kilkenny was.

A sour-faced man looked up from his beef and beans.

"Three against twenty-five or thirty?"

Swede Carlson shifted his weight. "I never did cotton to Havalik, and this fight's over. So if you need help, count on me."

"Thanks."

The sour-faced man spat. "I'll herd cattle."

Ben Tetlow had sat silent. Now he spoke up. "A man can get mighty saddle-sore trying to straddle a fence. I've made my play and I'm backing it. So I say this. If there's anybody here who figures to help Havalik or Andy, for that matter, he can ride out now. When trouble starts those who want can herd cattle. If any of you want to, you can lend a hand to Kilkenny. It's every man to his own conscience. I'll herd cattle. I couldn't draw a gun against my brother. One more thing. Anybody who decides to help Kilkenny, don't expect anything from Andy. When he starts shooting he ain't going to mind where his shots go. He's my brother, but I want no man to die because of that."

He walked away from the fire and Cain Brockman went to his bedroll and got out his extra gun. Few men could equal him with a pair of sixguns. Kilkenny had beaten him, but nobody else ever had.

Horns bobbing, the herd moved steadily north. Dust arose and filled the air. The lowing cattle and occasional shrill yells of the cowhands were the only other sounds. Kilkenny rode ahead, scouting the trail.

There was a tenseness in the air, an expectation. Cain rode lazily, but under his battered brim his eyes were ceaselessly moving.

If Havalik planned to hit the herd he would not do it until it was in the valley. If he had not learned the circumstances of Ben Tetlow's deal he would be puzzled by the personnel of the riders.

Yet there was no reason why he should hold off any attack on Kilkenny or his own riders.

Until the cattle reached the valley it was a Tetlow herd. Once there it belonged to Kilkenny and was fair game.

As the day drew on, Kilkenny grew increasingly restless and irritable. He rode far ahead of the herd, anxious to meet the issue and face it out. His eyes were never still and his nerves were on a hair trigger.

For the first time there was much at stake besides his own life, for now he had definitely committed himself and had bound, both in his own mind and in words, his future to that of Nita. Yet knowing the danger could not be avoided he wanted it to be now, quickly, and then over and done.

Cain Brockman, who knew his friend, watched him warily. When action came it would be explosive. Lance Kilkenny was a man who could be pushed only so far and Brockman could see that a devil was riding him.

Suddenly Kilkenny smelled dust in the air. He swung wide and saw the tracks of four riders where they had cut across the trail the herd was taking. He wheeled his buckskin and rode down the trail after them.

They were standing in a tight group not sixty yards off the trail, concealed from it by a rocky projection. As the buckskin walked in sand they did not hear his approach.

Kilkenny drew up, his right hand resting on his thigh. "Huntin' trouble or just riding?"

They jerked around, their faces written large with surprise. All four were tough men. "What's it to you?" The speaker was a big, wide-faced man.

Kilkenny's eyes had gone flat and hard. For three long breaths he did not reply. Nor did he think. He had it in him, and he felt something rising strong and hot inside him. He walked his horse nearer.

"You've been ridin' with Forty. This herd will be Forty until it reaches my ranch, but I won't have any saddle bums riding my flanks. If you think this is bluff, suppose you grab iron."

Silence hung heavy in the small canyon. The man who had spoken wanted to act, but he knew he looked into the eyes of death.

Fury mounted within Kilkenny. He stepped his horse nearer and, sensing his master's urgency, the buckskin began to tremble. "Come on, damn you! If you want trouble, start it! Otherwise start ridin' and don't stop until you're out of the country!"

The man with the wide face possessed his own fighting pride. Something exploded within him. "I'll be damned if I'll run! I'll—" He grabbed at his gun butt and Kilkenny slammed home the spurs.

The buckskin leaped like a startled rabbit and hit the other man's horse a glancing blow. Caught off balance, the horse staggered, then fell. And then Kilkenny was in the circle of horsemen, not shooting, but slashing with his gun barrel.

One man caught a blow across the skull and crumpled from his saddle. Another caught the tip of a raking blow that laid his cheek open. Wheeling his horse, he headed south at a dead run, blood steaming from his ripped face.

The man who had talked was struggling to get from under his horse. The remaining men backed off, hands in the air. His face was white, for he had never seen such berserk fury. "Lay off!" he yelled. "I ain't huntin' it!"

As suddenly as the fury had come, it was gone. "Get down there, and pull your partner from under that horse."

The fellow reached for his belt buckle. "That isn't necessary," Kilkenny told him. "Keep your guns. You might feel lucky."

Carefully the man got down from the saddle and catching the horse by the bridle he helped it up. The man who had tried for his gun lay on the sand. "You busted my leg!" he complained bitterly. "You busted it!"

"You're playing a rough game, amigo. Any time you draw chips you should figure what you can stand to lose."

Nevertheless, he swung down. "Let's get that leg set. Then you can come on to our camp. You're in no shape to travel."

Together they set the man's broken leg, and as they bound the splints the rider who had been knocked out began to groan. Kilkenny jerked his head toward him. "Get his gun. He might start shooting before he has a chance to think."

The rider hesitated. "You'll trust me to get his gun?" He was incredulous.

"You're tough," Kilkenny said, "but you aren't a damned fool!"

Kilkenny retrieved the fallen man's horse, then his own. The
man with the Mexican hat was holding his head in both hands.
"We'll start for camp. Listen, sorehead, you can make up your mind
whether you want trouble or ride away under your own power."

"Trouble?" The fellow looked up through eyes squinted with
pain. "I got trouble!"

"Mount up, then, and start for Horsehead."

It was evening when they reached the valley. The long sweep
of country lay before them, dotted now with streamers of mist.
Far away the mountains were a deep purple with evening except
their higher ridges which caught a hint of fire from the setting sun.

"Lord!" Tetlow breathed. "What a country!"

The herd flowed past them, and the heads of the cattle came
up, nostrils distended. After two days of driving they scented the
flowers, the grass, and the pines. They began to trot and then of
their own volition, as if knowing they were home, they began to
spread out and sink their muzzles in the grass. And then, faintly,
the wind stirred.

The cattle felt it, and the men. As if on signal they began to
listen. And the wind seemed to whisper faint words, not quite
discernible, and the cows moved on, ears wide, stopping from
time to time for a mouthful of grass.

"This is where I stop, Tetlow," Kilkenny said. "This is home."

Together the riders bunched and rode down the valley toward
the cabin, and there was silence among them.

At daylight the riders from the Forty rode away down the
valley, and only Cain Brockman and Shorty remained with
Kilkenny. There had been no sign of Havalik, nor of his men.

Two days later, riding among the cattle near the foot of the
range, Nita drew rein beside Kilkenny. "What now, Lance?" she
asked. "Us?"

"Not yet. First there's Dee Havalik."

"I see no reason to wait, Lance. I'm not afraid."

"You never were."

They walked their horses back to the ranch. Shorty was sitting on the top step whittling and he looked up as they drew near, then jerked his head at a stranger who stood near a saddled horse. "Tetlow wants to see you. He sent this gent."

Kilkenny studied the man, who was a stranger. "Heard anything from Havalik?"

"Not much," the rider admitted. "Most of the men left him. He's mighty mean. I rode with him myself, but he ain't fit to be around. Only one can get along with him is Andy Tetlow."

"How many men has he got?"

"Maybe six. He killed West. The others just drifted off when the chance offered."

"What's Tetlow want?"

"Never said. That jail's mighty hard on him."

Kilkenny tied the buckskin in front of the livery stable and left instructions for his care. Brockman did likewise, and then the two men crossed the bridge to east town.

Leal Macy got up with a quick smile as they entered. "Glad to see you, boys! Tetlow's been asking for you, Lance."

"How's everything?"

"Couldn't be better! Haven't had a fight in town in two weeks and business couldn't be better."

He opened the door to the cells and Kilkenny walked along until he came to that occupied by Tetlow. There had been no attempt at rescue by either Andy or Havalik, yet the old man was ramrod stiff. Ben had sent him tobacco despite his rebuffs. Now Tetlow came to the bars. "Didn't figure you'd come." There was no warmth in his voice.

Tetlow stood silent at the bars, and searching his face, Kilkenny could see no change in the man. If anything he had grown harder, colder. Yet there was a change. There was something cruel in his eyes, something cruel and somehow triumphant.

"I bought some of your cows from Ben. A nice lot."

"He'd no right to sell. Not to you, leastways."

"He stood his ground, played a man's part."

Kilkenny was puzzled. Jared Tetlow made no move to introduce whatever it was he wanted to discuss. He waited, giving the old man time.

"You'd better take care of that man Brockman," Tetlow said. "Andy figures to kill him along with you."

"He'd better leave Cain alone. Jared, you don't know about Cain. Neither does Andy. The man's hell on wheels."

He hesitated a moment longer. "What did you want to see me about?"

Jared Tetlow stared at him. Then he turned away. "Changed my mind," he said abruptly.

Kilkenny felt a little alarm bell ring in his brain. Carefully he turned his head and looked down the hall. At the end there was a small window, but there was no one in sight. And there was no one else around. He drew back from the bars, studying Tetlow.

His black coat was shabby and worn. There was a stubble of beard on his jaws. He looked mean . . . like a cornered, half-starved wolf.

"Then I'll go," Kilkenny said.

He had walked three paces and had a hand on the knob when Jared Tetlow spoke. "Maybe I just wanted to see how a man looks before he dies."

Kilkenny hesitated, his mind working swiftly. Then he stepped out and drew the door to behind him.

Macy looked up, but after a quick glance around the office Kilkenny walked past to the door. He stood there, looking up and down the street.

"What did he want?"

Without replying to the question, Kilkenny stepped out and then stopped abruptly. A man stood in the center of the bridge staring across the street from Kilkenny.

The man on the bridge was Andy Tetlow and he was staring at Cain Brockman.

Brockman stood in the shadow under the awning, bulking, ominous.

Andy Tetlow took a step forward, then spoke, his voice ringing with arrogance. "All right, Brockman!"

Cain Brockman stepped from under the awning. Two hundred and forty pounds of him, his big head lowered and thrust slightly forward, his thick hands swinging near his gun butts. He stepped into the street but he said nothing.

Kilkenny, who understood such things, saw that Tetlow was

surprised. Obviously, Havalik, who knew about Cain, had told Andy Tetlow nothing about the big man. It was apparent from Andy's attitude that he expected an easy kill, but there was no fear in the big man. He came out like a lion stalking game, easy on his feet, utterly dangerous.

"I'm going to kill you, Brockman!"

Andy Tetlow shouted, staring up the street at the big silent man. The realization that all was not as expected was revealed in that shouted statement when no statement was necessary.

Cain Brockman moved forward on cat feet and for the first time Andy Tetlow got the full weight of the menace that faced him. He saw for the first time that far from being frightened the big man accepted the fight with eagerness.

Instantly, Andy Tetlow took a step back and his hands dropped for his guns.

They dropped and they came up but even as his finger tightened on the trigger Brockman's gun flowered with flame and a bullet struck Andy in the shoulder, knocking him back a step and deflecting his aim. A second bullet smashed him in the chest and two drove through his stomach. He fired again, his bullet smashing into the bridge rail, and then Andy fell against the rail, fought for balance and finally got his feet under him. Dying, he turned blindly to face Cain Brockman, but the big man knew no mercy.

Guns hammering, he walked in. A bullet smashed Tetlow's knee, another ripped into his stomach and Tetlow fell back against the bridge railing, which gave way, and he fell heavily to the creek bed, twenty feet below.

As suddenly as the shooting had begun it was over. Leal Macy came running to stand beside Kilkenny and Brockman, looking down at the bullet-riddled body. Blood stained the small creek and the water washed around the body, turning dark the dead man's clothing.

"This country," a bystander said, "is mighty hard on Tetlows. They'd better find a different climate."

"Watch yourself." Brockman looked around. "He wouldn't have been alone."

Kilkenny had been thinking the same thing. It was all very plain now. Jared Tetlow had sent for him to set him up in the right alley for the guns of Havalik. Dee and Andy had divided the work between them, only Dee had not let Andy know what he was facing. It was just like the man.

"We'll need a couple of pack horses," Kilkenny said. "I want to take more supplies home. I'll get Buck."

Kilkenny turned on his heel and walked across the bridge toward the center of town. Doc Blaine, drawn to his door by the shooting, stood talking to Laurie Webster. About Dolan's there was an air of bustle and business. Men loitered on the steps at Savory's, and Kilkenny gave them a quick glance before he entered the big livery stable.

It was cool inside and there was a pleasant barn-like smell of hay, manure, and horses. A horse stomped in a stall and blew contentedly through his nose. Several horses rolled their eyes back at him, showing the whites. There was no one about as he led Buck to the trough, then went back through the barn and into the wide corral.

Behind this corral was a wagon yard, and to the left of that, another corral. It was in that corral where Dolan kept his stock.

Trees walled both the corral from which he had come and the wagon yard, and the latter was filled with huge old ore wagons. Two freight wagons stood in the center of the yard, not together, and five others stood, tongues pointing high, in a row. Others lined the sides of the yard.

Men had been greasing the wagons and preparing them for use, but they had gone to eat and the yard was lifeless and still in the hot noonday sun.

Kilkenny closed the gate and was about to cross the yard to the other corral when a boot scraped. Instantly he froze in position, every sense alert.

The air was very still. The dust was warm. Cottonwood leaves brushed their polished palms together. He listened, but there was no other sound. Stepping quickly into the shelter of a huge freight wagon, he dropped to his haunches and studied the yard through the spokes of a high wheel.

At first there was no sound of movement, and then through the myriad spokes of other lined up wheels, he caught a glint of sunlight on a spur!

He dried his palms on his jeans. His sun-browned face was still and cold, his eyes a deeper green. He pulled his hat brim a little lower and touched his gun butts, loosening them in the holsters. He saw the boots again, and the neat, small feet.

Havalik . . .

Rising swiftly, Kilkenny turned and ran lightly and swiftly to the wagons along the corral fence. Ducking behind them, he could see the wagon where Havalik had been. The gunman was gone.

Kilkenny hesitated, studying the situation. The corral comprised approximately an acre of ground, and in it were at least thirty wagons. Kilkenny decided that Havalik had seen him, had been stalking him, and was now about where Kilkenny had been before. Also, Havalik was not aware the trap had failed.

Kilkenny squatted and peered through the spokes. A bullet smashed within inches of his face, stinging it with tiny splinters, and a shot sounded in the stillness of the corral.

He sprang back, and his spring sent him toppling off-balance to the ground. A second bullet nailed the hub of the big wheel near his face, splattering him with fresh grease. Lunging to his feet, Kilkenny ran around the end of the wagon at the same instant Havalik rounded another wagon thirty yards distant. Both men fired.

Havalik's bullet tugged at Kilkenny's shirt collar and Dee sprang to shelter, apparently unhurt.

Kilkenny called out, "In the open, Dee! Let's settle this now!"

There was no reply. Behind him he heard movement. He turned swiftly and saw Dave, one of Havalik's men, with a shotgun at his shoulder. Kilkenny fired and the shotgun bellowed, but Kilkenny's shot had been fired as a man points a finger. The swing, the point in one unceasing movement. The bullet drilled Dave through the shirt pocket and his knees buckled, throwing the charge of shot harmlessly into the air.

Instantly, Kilkenny sprang and grabbed the wagontop, swinging over the edge and dropping soundlessly into the wagon. He crouched there, listening. The last report gave Havalik six men.

Andy Tetlow was gone. And now Dave.

He waited, letting them look for him. Through a crack in the side of the wagon he saw nobody, so he swung over to the ground again. Seeing movement, he rounded the wagon.

Dee Havalik was moving across the open, but seeing him Dee

stopped and swung to meet him. Under the old gray hat Havalik's eyes seemed to blaze with malignant fire. Kilkenny saw the guns come up, lining on his belt, and then both men fired at once.

A bullet tugged at his shirt, and he saw Havalik flinch.

Kilkenny ran straight at Havalik, his guns ready. Havalik lifted his gun to shoot, but the charging man was too much for him and he broke ground. Instantly Kilkenny skidded to a halt and dropping to one knee he shot three times as fast as he could slip the hammer off his thumb. The bullets slammed into Havalik and he backed up, cursing. His gray face was suddenly livid with a red gash where his lips had been. The red grew and blood trickled from both corners of his mouth. Havalik fired and the bullet burned Kilkenny's ribs and Kilkenny fired again.

He saw Havalik jerk as the bullet struck him in the belt and the gunman seemed to shrink, his face twisting. He fired again, and Kilkenny snapped a shot with his left-hand gun at the gun barrel that showed through the spokes of a wheel.

Then he walked around Havalik, forcing the wounded man to turn. When he got around on his left side he fired again and saw the bullet strike dust from the man's ribs in front of his drawn-back arm.

Havalik went down then, cursing bitterly. He tried to get up, failed, and fell face down on the hard-packed earth.

The echoes lost themselves against the hills and Lance Kilkenny stood erect and still in the open yard, looking carefully around him.

It was very hot. A trickle of sweat moved down his cheek. He heard a big fly buzz heavily in the sun. Leaves rustled . . . and then there was movement and he turned swiftly.

Havalik was on his feet, swaying drunkenly, his clothing smeared with blood and dust. Kilkenny fired and the bullet smashed Havalik in the teeth. He fell flat on his face, all sprawled out, and did not move again.

A man sprang from hiding and lunged at the fence. He was too slow, for as he grasped the top of the fence and swung himself over, Kilkenny snapped a quick shot that knocked him loose from his hold and he hit the ground on the far side, leaving a finger behind him.

Cain Brockman came into the wagon yard and with him were Dolan, Early, and Macy.

Kilkenny walked to his horse and, mounting, rode up the street to the Pinenut where he went inside for a quick drink. When he came out Cain sat his horse, holding the lead ropes of two packed horses. Kilkenny mounted and the two men rode out of town.

Nita saw them coming and rode to meet them. Cain rode on ahead, but Kilkenny waited for her. When she rode up to him he said, "Honey, there's a minister in Horsehead. I think we should go see him."

Her eyes searched his face. "Then . . . it's over?"

"All over."

"Was . . . was it very bad?"

"Dee was in too much of a hurry."

They rode on in silence, their hands joined. Then he stopped abruptly and pulled her to him. Their bodies came together as their horses stopped side by side, and his lips touched hers and melted into welcoming softness, and he felt a strange fire thread through his veins.

And then the wind came, moving among the pines and then down the long grass levels where the cattle grazed, rippling the tall grass into changing gray and green and silver, and the horses pricked their ears, listening. It was very quiet then, in the Valley of the Whispering Wind.

Only the wind itself, whispering words of endearment to its first people.

7-03·00